A HIGH

JOHNNY OR___ ___ish-American, part Apache and all cop. In New Mexico's landscape of vast wilderness and ancient lore, he'll track a suspect through hell and back . . .

LUCILLE AND WALDO HARRINGTON— Charlie Harrington's brilliant physicist parents whose love of science seems stronger than their feelings for their son. Now he's dead, and they've turned their cold logic to finding his killer . . .

ROSS CATHCART—A high-rolling commodities trader whose sleazy deals, old grudges and wayward wife give him multiple motives for murder . . .

CASSIE ENRIGHT—Johnny's beloved, beautiful *chica,* a brilliant anthropologist with the courage to confront a dangerous man . . .

PENNY LINCOLN—The struggling artist's body brings a higher price than her paintings ever will. She's the last link in Charlie's chain of women . . .

CONGRESSMAN MARK HAWLEY—The tough old politico is pulling every string he can to control Johnny's investigation . . .

BEN HART—The bourbon-belting rancher has a bear's temper, a kind heart—and a dead man on his north forty . . .

TANGLED MURDERS

"Johnny Ortiz is a welcome new addition to the lists of the great detectives. I hope we see a lot more of him."

—Hillary Waugh

RICHARD MARTIN STERN

POCKET BOOKS

New York   London   Toronto   Sydney   Tokyo

This is a work of fiction and it does not portray, nor is it
intended to portray, any actual person, living or dead. If the
characters seem real, I am flattered, because they are purely
creatures of invention.

An *Original* Publication of POCKET BOOKS

 POCKET BOOKS, a division of Simon & Schuster Inc.
1230 Avenue of the Americas, New York, NY 10020

Copyright © 1988 by Richard Martin Stern
Cover artwork copyright © 1988 Ron Lesser

ISBN: 0-671-65260-5

First Pocket Books printing January 1989

10 9 8 7 6 5 4 3 2 1

POCKET and colophon are trademarks of
Simon & Schuster Inc.

Printed in the U.S.A.

For D.A.S.
with love always

TANGLED MURDERS

1

There had been no rain within the last twenty-four hours, which was a factor to be considered as they stood looking down at the crumpled body in the overgrown and unused irrigation ditch.

Sergeant Tony Lopez, large, solid, and usually imperturbable, crossed himself. *"Madre de Dios!"* He said it in a near whisper. "Somebody wanted him dead, but good!"

Johnny—Lieutenant Juan Felipe Ortiz, Apache on his mother's side and, as far as he knew, part-Anglo and part-Spanish on his father's—nodded agreement, remembering another body in similar condition after a riot gun had been fired at point-blank range and without hesitation by a very proper, sixty-year-old gentleman from Boston wearing a seersucker suit, button-down shirt, bow tie, and immaculate black loafers. That riot-gun blast had saved Johnny's life.

9

Memories, sometimes but not always extraneous, Johnny thought, popped up without warning out of depths ordinarily unplumbed, hidden.

Tony Lopez, looking more closely now, said, "He's barefoot. And in this mess of chamisa, even some prickly pear?" He shook his head. "No way."

"He wasn't shot here," Johnny said, the memory of that other occasion clear and distinct and now measured automatically against the bone-dry brush. "Not enough blood." His tone was final. "Call Doc Means. We'll want him to have a look before we touch anything."

He waited, studying the scene carefully until Tony came back from Johnny's pickup and the radio. "Who reported it?" Johnny said then.

Tony consulted his notebook. "Kids out hunting a lost dog found the body. They ran home to report. Fortunata Romero called it in, the mother of one of the kids." He closed the notebook and added unnecessarily, "Nobody saw anything. Nobody heard anything. Nobody knows anything. A dead Anglo in this neighborhood could mean trouble."

Johnny nodded. *"Claro."* He was measuring distance and sounded preoccupied. "Easy enough," he said at last. "Car stops here on the pavement. Whoever gets out, takes the body out of the car and pushes or drops it in the ditch. No need to step off the pavement."

"Pity," Tony said. "Not even one footprint." Tony had heard it said of Johnny—and was prepared to believe—that "that damned Indian would track a man through hell and out the other side, and then stake him out on an anthill."

"So we start without a starting place," Johnny said. He was smiling faintly, without amusement.

"Except," Tony said, "that we know who he is, *amigo.*"

"Oh, yes, we have that. And it merely complicates things."

Doc Means was in his early seventies, Santo Cristo's dollar-a-year forensic-pathologist-coroner, in happy retirement from a similar but more formal, far better-paying, and more prestigious job in the East. He looked down at the body and echoed Tony's opinion. "Somebody wanted him dead, and no mistake. Shotgun blast at close range tends to be conclusive." He looked at Johnny. "Recognize him?"

"Unfortunately, yes. And there's going to be a stink." Johnny's voice was uninflected. "His name is, was Charley Harrington."

"And many folks," Tony Lopez said, "are going to think it couldn't have happened to a nicer guy."

Johnny nodded in reluctant agreement. His face was inscrutable. "But that won't prevent the stink. He was an important fellow."

"Young-looking," Doc Means said.

Johnny nodded again. "Just turned twenty-two, I think. But he began making his mark locally when he was about fourteen." He had one last look. "Can we move him?"

"If you can gather him up," Doc Means said. "I've seen all I need."

It was October. At ancient Santo Cristo's 7,000-foot elevation, the evenings and mornings were cool-to-

11

chilly, light jacket or sweater time, and after dark a fire in the fireplace was welcome and cheery even though heat from trompe walls, forced-air furnaces, or baseboard radiators was already providing its engineered comfort.

On the slopes of the great mountains behind the city—timberline at this latitude is 11,500 feet—the aspens had already turned gold. They glowed in masses amid the solemn green of the Ponderosa pine forest.

The first snows would come shortly, and from that time through April or even May, the tops of Lake Peak and Baldy, well over 12,000 feet, would glisten in the sun, and on clear moonlit nights give off their near-luminescence against the darker sky as if their snow cover were lighted from within.

There would be hopes for early skiing by Thanksgiving, but mid-to-late December would be the better guess, and so, although there were always tourists in the old city, it was not yet swarming with visitors.

Johnny sat in his office, and Tony Lopez leaned his solid bulk against the wall to listen. Johnny would talk, Tony knew, as if to himself, in reality throwing out ideas for them both to consider. Tony did not pretend to comprehend the way Johnny's mind worked. Tony was pure Hispanic, and to him the Indian part of Johnny smacked of unknown visions and insights best left unquestioned.

"Charley Harrington," Johnny said now, and let the name hang in the air. It vibrated with overtones.

"A pain in the ass from the start," Tony said as if reciting his catechism.

"Close enough." Johnny was staring at the wall, unseeing. "I first heard of him when he was about fourteen, like I said to Doc." He smiled faintly, remembering. "What they call, I think, a hacker, playing games with his personal computer." The smile spread as he looked at Tony. "He broke into and loused up a part of the Scientific Lab's computer memory that had to do, I heard, with research on controlled nuclear fusion—hydrogen bomb stuff. Just for the hell of it."

"They hushed it up," Tony said.

"They hushed up a lot of things. He got into the interstate bank's computer network with a dummy corporation name and set up a drawing account with the bank's money." Johnny shook his head in remembered wonder. "A hell of a bright kid, maybe a genius. Parents like that—" Waldo and Lucille Harrington, world-class physicists. "Charley was fifteen or so then," Johnny said, "and he used the money to develop in the garage a new kind of personal computer compatible with IBM, Apple, Commodore and some that hadn't even come out yet. CH Company, he called it, and a year ago he sold it to some conglomerate, I forget the name, for more loot than Cortez took out of Mexico."

Tony was silent, wondering what it would be like to have more money than you could comfortably count. The concept was disquieting.

"And now he's dead," Johnny said. "We have a good idea how, but we don't know where, and we don't know why."

"Little things like that," Tony said, and dismissed them with a wave of one large hand. "Mere details."

"Who would want him dead?" Johnny said.

This Tony could answer. "Half the population of Santo Cristo County. You've only covered part of him, *amigo*. There are those reckless-driving charges, those rapes, other little things, all while he was still a juvenile." Tony was silent for a moment or two. "And all of them—like you said, hushed up or at least charges dropped." Again he was silent. "Anglos," he said at last, biting off the word and looking as if he wanted to spit.

Johnny was looking up at Tony with fresh interest now. "Those girls—Hispanic?"

"No. Give him that. Always Anglo. He never risked a knife in the belly going after some poor Spanish kid's girl."

"So let's start there," Johnny said. "As a kid he was a stud. Chances are he didn't change."

Tony sighed. "You want a list? Like a box score?"

"This is your town," Johnny said. "You're related to half of it. Ask around and see what you can find."

Johnny sat on motionless after Tony had gone, staring at the blank wall, letting his thoughts run as they would.

Waldo and Lucille Harrington, parents. Johnny doubted that they could cast any light because their relationship with their son, or lack of relationship, was common knowledge. But they had to be notified regardless.

Johnny called the National Scientific Lab, talked briefly, and hung up. Waldo was in Japan on some kind of scientific conference; Lucille was in Washington testifying before some congressional committee.

Johnny pushed his chair back suddenly and stood up. He disliked walls around him and the sense of being enclosed. Outside in the crisp fall air was much better. He could breathe. And it came as no surprise that his footsteps automatically turned toward the museum where Cassie worked. Cassie was always a place to start.

Cassie was in—Cassandra Enright, Ph.D., anthropologist, tall, stunningly rounded, with Caucasian features and *café-au-lait* skin. Once, in a moment of rare, openly exposed weakness, she had said to old Congressman Mark Hawley, "I'm a black chick with a go-go dancer's carcass and a head stuffed to the eyeballs with anthropological erudition, and where am I going to find a man to go with all that?"

And the congressman had said, "Honey, if I were thirty years younger—"

"You'd ruin your career." Cassie was smiling again.

What the congressman said then brought tears to Cassie's eyes despite the smile. "You'd be worth it." And there was no mistaking the conviction in his voice, which only made the tears harder to control.

Now, in a flannel shirt with sleeves rolled up on her slim arms, jeans, and cowboy boots—her customary working costume—she sat at her desk and smiled as Johnny came in. "Hi. You skipped breakfast, just dressed and split. What's up?"

Johnny sat down in the visitor's chair and told her, while his fingers automatically rubbed the ears of the collie-shepherd-huskie-mix dog who had appeared from beneath the desk.

"A waste," was Cassie's reaction when he had finished, "a terrible waste. A horror, but he could have been one of the great ones."

"Somebody didn't bother to think of that, *chica.* Somebody just wanted him good and dead."

"Do you think it was planned, or just spur-of-the-moment?" Cassie understood her role. Catalyst, she had often thought; by idle, even seemingly fatuous questions she sometimes had the power to start a chain reaction. Warm knowledge.

"Folks don't usually walk around carrying scatter-guns, *chica*. They're hard to hide. And they make big bangs when they go off." He grinned at his own words. "I'm already setting limits, no? Maybe the *where* is the key."

"What kind of people use shotguns?"

"No." Johnny shook his head. "There's nothing there. This is hunting country. Too many long guns to count. Too many knives and handguns too, as far as that goes, and too many crazies who use them."

"He was terribly rich, if we can believe the papers."

"Robbery? With violence?" Johnny shook his head. "He probably didn't carry cash. Not many do. His signature was good anywhere in town. Or a credit card. Robberies happen to *turistas,* and not with shotguns."

"Who knew him well?" Cassie said.

Johnny stared at her as if he had never seen her before, and his fingers on the dog's ears were suddenly stilled. "Bingo!" he said. "I should have thought of it myself."

"Who?"

Johnny was already on his feet. "Sid Thomas," he said, "and don't ask me why, because they couldn't have been more different."

Johnny parked his pickup on the winding road outside the studio of Sid Thomas, unofficial dean of Santo Cristo's considerable body of artists. Sid was well into his seventies and suffering from emphysema which Santo Cristo's high, clear, thin air did nothing to help, but all efforts to persuade Sid to move down to the veteran's hospital in the city 2,000 feet below had come to nothing.

"I'd rather live six weeks here," Sid had been known to declare, "than six years down in that money-grubbing imitation metropolis." Both Sid's convictions *and* his antic tendencies were still intact.

"Set, son," he told Johnny now. "It's time I took a little breather anyway. And a fix." He settled into his worn leather chair and sucked contemplatively on his oxygen bottle as he listened. And when Johnny was done, Sid shook his head sadly.

"No real surprise," he said, "but I'm sorry to hear it. In a way he'd been asking for it for a long time, no doubt about that."

"You're one of the few who knew him," Johnny said. "I mean *knew*. And I never understood why."

The fringe of white hair around Sid's tanned bald pate was perpetually rumpled and frequently paint-stained. He rumpled it a bit more now. "That's a tough one," he said. "It just—happened. Waldo and Lucille lived just up the street, renting, while they built the place they have now. Charley was just a kid." He sucked contemplatively on his oxygen. "Only he wasn't a kid. I don't know anything about kids. I don't know what to say to them without sounding like—what was his name?—Uncle Wiggly or one of those TV fellers always giving advice, you know what I mean?"

Johnny merely nodded.

"Charley," Sid Thomas said, "didn't need advice and wouldn't have taken it if I'd handed it to him. He already knew a lot of things I'll never know. But he'd never seen painting, I mean palette and brushes and mixing colors and things like that. He'd watch, and

17

he'd ask questions. Why this? Why that? 'You're exaggerating,' he'd say, and he'd squint at the canvas for a long spell and then shake his head. 'But, you're right. It looks more *real* like that, doesn't it?' All serious and interested. He sort of grew on me." Sid was silent for a few moments, the oxygen tube hanging loose in his hand, forgotten.

Johnny was silent too, and motionless with that bone-bred patience of his.

"He went with me down to the Fine Arts Museum and some of the galleries quite a few times," Sid said. "We just walked around, and looked. I didn't try to tell him anything. He wouldn't have liked that. But sometimes he'd ask questions, and I'd answer them best I could. 'How can they paint what isn't really there?' he'd say, 'And yet when you look at it, you see things you've never seen before.' Or, 'How can it be, in only two dimensions and on maybe a two-foot-by-three canvas, you see Lake Peak, twelve thousand, four hundred feet high, all of it?' That kind of thing." Sid shook his head. "He always wanted answers, but he knew answers aren't ever complete." He looked at Johnny. "You know what I mean?"

"I'm not sure."

Sid sucked oxygen while he thought about it. "He was into mathematics," he said, "way far beyond anything I could understand. Even then, I mean. He talked sometimes about things like the Uncertainty Principle, whatever that is, and quantum mechanics, which isn't arithmetic the way I learned it. He told me once, 'You can't explain art, nobody can, really pin it down and say, "There it is." I like that, because mathematics is probabilities too, not certainty.' I'm still not sure exactly what he meant, except that I guess we saw things kind of the same way."

Johnny said gently, "I think I'm beginning to understand." He was silent for a moment, turning it over in his mind. "Even after they moved away, you saw him, no? Did he ever talk about—enemies?"

Sid worked on the white fringe of hair for a little time while he thought about it. "He knew he didn't fit," he said at last. "Lots don't, no matter how hard they try. He didn't even try. I don't think he cared much one way or the other, but he looked at everybody like they were strangers, warylike, so maybe they were all—enemies."

"Except you," Johnny said.

Sid had a final pull on the oxygen and stood up with effort. "Back to work, son. The time I got left ain't, like the feller said, infinite. But you can set and talk. Won't bother me a mite."

The canvas on the easel, Johnny noticed, was beginning to display a single corner of the ancient Palace of the Governors. He stared hard at it, remembering what Sid had said. The angle *was* exaggerated, but the painted adobe-brick corner was already real enough to lean against in the cool shadow. "Thanks, Sid," he said, and got a wave of the brush in response.

He next drove back downtown and out to the state police lab to see Saul Pentland.

Saul, ex-NFL defensive tackle, bearded, with the face of an ancient prophet, big as a bear in his white coat and as impressive, said, "You want to know what we've found out, and the answer is just about zilch. Young Harrington is dead. You already know that. You saw what was left of him. Double-ought buckshot

19

and almost certainly both barrels of a twelve gauge at close range . . ."

He spread his huge hands.

"Double-ought," Johnny said. "Somebody wasn't going duck shooting then, or even after geese." He was silent, thinking about it. "That shirt of his," he said then, "all those pockets. Anything in it? Was he a note-taker?"

"All right here and inventoried," Saul said. "Help yourself."

Charley Harrington had indeed been a note-taker. Aside from ballpoint pens of various colors, credit cards, and driver's license, there were pages from a small notebook stuffed here and there within the many shirt pockets, seemingly without order. Some of the pages were torn and bloodstained by the shotgun blast, but many were legible, either mathematical symbols and numbers, or notes in a personal form of shorthand, easy enough to decipher.

"Hghr brk pdl," one read, and Johnny translated it without difficulty.

"The way he drove and used his brakes," he said, "I'd say a high brake pedal was only sensible."

"L&W re ins," read another, and on this one Johnny puzzled a bit.

"Of course, of course," he said at last, "Lucille and Waldo about insurance. His parents. But insurance on what? Or whom?" He shook his head. "They aren't even here to ask."

Saul's ancient-prophet face turned grave with sudden concern. "Have they been notified?"

Johnny nodded. "They'll come back separately as fast as they can break free." He hesitated. "But I somehow get the impression that Lucille and Waldo

20

pretty well gave up on Charley some time ago. What they produced was a monster-genius, and I think even a lonely, love-starved mother, let alone a pair of very busy world-class physicists, both male and female, would find that pretty hard to put up with." He paused. "Still," he added.

He gathered up the notes and the small notebook, along with the ballpoint pens, credit cards, and license. "I'll take these along for study, if you don't mind. I'll sign a receipt."

"Already made out," Saul said. He watched Johnny sign and then straighten with a question on his face. "Yes?"

"Possibly an accident?" Johnny said.

"Possible. Personally, I doubt it. His reputation—"

"Claro," Johnny said. He dismissed the matter of Harrington's reputation with a short, sharp gesture. "Shot from the front?"

"Or a slight front angle. Impossible to be certain."

"So," Johnny said, "he had a good look at who it was." He shook his head almost angrily, silently scolding himself. "Unless it was dark," he added, which merely posed one more imponderable to a puzzle that as yet had no handle. "See you," he said, and waved a hand as he walked out.

2

The next stop, he decided as he drove back into town, was the Santo Cristo unit of the fourteen-state-bank network. Bert Clancy, president, was in and available. Bert was a genial type, well-known and well-thought-of in Santo Cristo, large, rumpled, wearing heeled boots with his dark suit. A Fort Worth stetson hung on the coat rack in the corner.

"Since, in a manner of speaking," Johnny said, "Charley Harrington began with your bank, I assume he stayed on when he got around to putting money in instead of sneaking it out by computer?"

Bert smiled faintly and nodded. The computer theft was a painful subject. "Charley was a customer."

"Any money problems once he got started?"

"Charley," Bert said, "had problems the way a dog has fleas, but money wasn't one of them. Mind telling me what you're looking for?"

"A starting place."

Bert was silent for a moment. Then, "Charley," he said thoughtfully, "had the lovable disposition of a gila monster. His problems were people-problems. I don't think he even liked himself." He was silent again, contemplative. "Or maybe," he said, "he just didn't bother to think about liking or not liking anybody. He was kind of the way our computers are. He just went ahead no matter who thought what. You ever try to argue with a computer?"

"Not successfully."

"Then you know what I mean. They don't pay any attention to you. They just blink their lights and spin their wheels and ignore everything and everybody."

It fitted with Sid's assessment, Johnny thought, and merely nodded. "Building that company of his," he said, "took a lot of money. The bank financed him?"

Bert picked up a pencil and fiddled with it for a little time, keeping his eyes on it as if it were important. He looked up at last. "Not—intentionally," he said, and showed obvious embarrassment at Johnny's quick grin. "Uh," Bert said, "goddamnit, Johnny, we suspected him. We'd have been even bigger damn fools than we look if we hadn't. But every time we managed to catch up with him, he had already accomplished what he wanted, and was sweet as pie and paid us back without any question."

"So you never pressed charges?"

Bert opened his mouth with every intention of explaining the situation in detail, changed his mind and said merely, "We never pressed charges. Holding-company decision." His embarrassment had deepened. "Made me personally look like a damn fool, but—" He spread his hands. "Like they say, it goes with the territory." His tone changed. "But there was one thing."

"Yes?"

"There were discrepancies. You can fool good accountants for a time, but sooner or later they can put it all together. Definite discrepancies."

"Let me get this straight," Johnny said. "You mean you didn't get back all he had managed to finagle?"

Bert shook his head emphatically. "That's not it at all. We got back every penny every time, with interest when that seemed right. The discrepancies—maybe I ought to say *apparent* discrepancies—were in what he did with the money because he always *seemed* to have put more into his CH Company than he had hornswoggled out of us. And nobody knew where he got the difference."

Johnny was again unable to stifle his grin. "He seems to have been a couple of steps ahead of everybody."

Bert Clancy shook his head in slow wonderment. "If he'd taken it in his head to go East, Wall Street, he'd have made those insider-information fellows look like pikers. But all he cared about was his CH Company, building it and finally selling it."

Johnny was frowning now. "Any idea why? I'm talking about motivation."

"I'm a country banker," Bert Clancy said. "I'm not a shrink."

Johnny's next stop, which, he told himself, by the book probably ought to have been his first, was Charley Harrington's house.

It was old, adobe, and not large, perched alone and high on the mountain slope above town with a stunning view of the great peaks behind it marching northward into the distance; of the two other mountain groupings surrounding the old city; and off to the west-southwest, sharp and clear on the horizon in the October air, the solitary peak of Mount Taylor, which was, as Johnny knew, over 100 air miles distant. He wondered if Charley Harrington had ever studied the view, or if his apparent almost total introspection prevented him from noticing the grandeur that had been his to admire.

But it was clear that the house itself had been a focus of Charley's attention, because thoroughly modern and ingeniously camouflaged solar collectors had been installed, and despite the growing chill of the late-afternoon outside air, the interior of the house was snug and warm. No local architect Johnny knew was capable of that kind of ingenuity; it smacked of C. Harrington.

There were other things too that caught Johnny's eye, and began to round out the picture of the dead man he had known only by reputation.

One entire wall of the living room was bookcases, built-in and filled, not only with technical and scientific books which might have been expected, but also with so-called mainstream novels; science fiction and mystery-suspense; cheek-by-jowl with a few biographies, books on economics and history; the compact edition of the *OED* as well as the unabridged *Webster's New International Dictionary,* Second Edition; the *Columbia Encyclopedia;* both *Bartlett's* and the *Oxford Dictionary of Quotations* as well as an up-to-date edition of *Black's Law Dictionary* . . . . Charley Harrington, Johnny thought, had wider interests than one might have guessed.

By the age of fifteen, Johnny remembered hearing,

Charley had turned down scholarship offers from both MIT and Cal Tech, apparently considering his own brand of self-education better than anything offered elsewhere and refusing to travel to such distant spots as Cambridge, Massachusetts or Pasadena, California to prove it.

The Indian rugs on the brick floors were of top quality, Johnny noted, and the furniture was heavy, hand-crafted locally, and upholstered in consistently good, quiet taste, earth tones relieved by touches of black—traditional, to harmonize with the rugs.

A combination turntable, amplifier, tuner, and tape recorder stood against another wall, and the two massive speakers suspended from the vigas of the ceiling were of a design Johnny had never seen, even in the state-of-the-art magazines Cassie loved to pore over.

The bedroom was sparsely but tastefully furnished with an oversize bed possibly planned with dalliance in mind, a hand-crafted nine-drawer dresser, a single straight chair, and, over the bed, a highly functional reading lamp with rheostat control. A single huge rug, without doubt custom-woven in a pleasing geometric design, covered almost the entire floor.

The closet and the drawers contained a jumble of jeans, sweaters, shirts, boots, and outer clothing for winter, but nothing even vaguely resembling neckties, tailored jackets, or trousers, items Charley Harrington had obviously not considered necessary.

Off the bedroom was Charley's study, the large desk piled high with papers, one of his own computers and printers handy, along with an electric typewriter, a neat vertical desk-rack of bond paper, second sheets, and graph paper, a stein in the shape of a skull holding pencils and pens, and a complicated desk calculator with, aside from the usual numbers, key symbols Johnny could only wonder at.

He walked back out into the living room and stood for a time looking around, having no idea what, if anything, he might be searching for. In reality, as he admitted to himself, he was merely trying to absorb the atmosphere and something of the flavor of Charley Harrington.

The kitchen was neat, efficient—quite possibly also Charley's design, Johnny decided—and without character, a place intended merely as a workshop for preparing food, and probably very simple types of food at that.

From the kitchen, a passageway with a tiled and polished floor—curiously different from the brick flooring throughout the rest of the house—led to the double garage.

There were two cars, a blood-red Ferrari roadster, polished and immaculate, and a well-used Toyota Land Cruiser with oversize heavy-treaded tires, no doubt for use in winter or for forays into the mountains. There were no keys in either vehicle, and the automatic overhead garage door was closed and locked.

Johnny stood for quite a time surveying the scene and thinking about it. Along one wall of the garage was a workbench, and hand tools neatly hung on a pegboard from hooks and brackets. A pair of cross-country skis and poles stood in a corner, but beyond these, there were no impedimenta indicating that outdoor activities had played a role in Charley Harrington's life. Incongruously, a scuffed pair of loafers rested on the floor beside the skis.

Thinking done and conclusion reached, Johnny went back into the house and used the phone in the kitchen to call the state police lab and Saul Pentland. While he waited for the call to be completed, he kept staring contemplatively at the polished, tiled floor of the passageway, and when Saul's deep voice came on the line, Johnny said, "I'm playing a hunch, Saul. How's to come over here to the Harrington house? I'll wait."

He walked back into the living room and, merely killing time, studied the stereo system which seemed, as one might expect, complicated, expensive, and no doubt superb. There was even—he identified this only after rejecting several other guesses—a laser-operated disc player, something he had not seen up close before. And on the top of what was clearly a record cabinet was a small loose-leaf notebook, with recordings neatly and alphabetically identified by composer or artist, and numbered; an eclectic selection. He thumbed through idly, finding, among others, J.P. Johnson and Fats Waller, Joe Sullivan, Earl Hines, Artur Rubenstein, Rudolph Serkin, Heinz Holliger, Henryk Szerying, and conductors of the caliber of Ormandy, Bernstein, Ashkenazy, and Barenboim performing Bach, Handel, Haydn, Beethoven, Mozart, Dvořák. . . .

He was leafing through a copy of *Scientific American* when Saul drove up and pounded on the front door. Johnny went to meet him. "Let me show you through the house," he said, and that was all.

After the tour they settled again in the living room. Johnny waited in silence, not wanting to influence Saul's thinking.

"The garage was added," Saul said. "So?"

"So was that tiled hallway from the kitchen to the garage."

Saul nodded approvingly. "Smart, that. You come in, maybe from that Land Cruiser in winter, snowy or muddy boots. Tile cleans easily, whereas brick—" He stopped. "Oh," he said, and searched Johnny's face.

"The garage door is locked," Johnny said. "Those electronic doors lock themselves when they go down. There are no keys in either car. And I didn't see one of those hand-audio signals to operate the door, so maybe Harrington had some fancy switch in each car. It would be like him, I think." He felt he was beginning to know Charley Harrington.

"Go on," Saul said.

"*Bueno*. He gets out of whichever car and starts into the house, and somebody's waiting to blast him right there in that tiled hallway. How about that? The mess could be cleaned up, no? Like you said, tile is easy to clean. And then the body was moved?"

Saul sat motionless, in deep thought. Wordlessly, he got up and walked back out to the kitchen to stand studying the tiled floor of the passageway and the walls of smooth white plaster. Johnny waited behind him.

"Could be," Saul said at last. "Isolated up here, nobody to hear a shotgun blast, probably plenty of time to clean up the mess." He turned then to face Johnny. "We'll find out," he said, and his face was set now, angry. "Cleaning up blood isn't as easy as it looks without leaving traces of some kind. And if there are traces, we'll find them."

"It's all yours," Johnny said. "Search the house while you're about it, and then seal it, huh?"

Saul's face was unrelenting, that of a vengeful prophet. "You got it."

3

Johnny had a visitor waiting when he got back to his office. In the room outside Tony Lopez handed him the visitor's card: Joseph R. Whitney, Attorney at Law.

"You know him, don't you?" Tony said.

"I've seen him around."

"Old family," Tony said. "Real old. Been here forever."

"Joe Whitney," the visitor said and held out his hand when Johnny walked in. "I've heard a lot about you, Lieutenant." He had an easy smile.

Johnny shook hands briefly and sat down. "Small town," he said, and waited. A confident man, Whitney, he thought, in good shape and bigger than he would have guessed from seeing him on the street. Anglo, but maybe with a touch of Spanish too in those brown eyes. So?

"I've been out of town," Whitney said. "Just got back and heard about Charley Harrington." His smile was suddenly gone and he shook his head with slow gravity. "Terrible thing. Too much of that these days. Any ideas?" The easy smile reappeared quickly. "Not just idle curiosity, Lieutenant. I was Charley's attorney, and he named me as co-executor of his will. So I have what you might call a legitimate interest."

"Will," Johnny said, and was surprised that he had not even thought of it before. The trouble, of course, was that in Santo Cristo most homicides had to do with men, or women, who had never even considered such things as wills because they usually had little, if anything, to make a will about. Charley Harrington was a different matter entirely, and that opened up all sorts of new possibilities.

"I can't give you details without going through the legal motions, Lieutenant, but the bulk of Charley's estate will go to the setting up of a Charles Harrington Foundation, the aims of which were carefully spelled out in the trust agreement that will establish it."

"Charles Harrington Foundation," Johnny said, and was silent for a little time thinking about it. Then, "Those things have to be organized, no? Trustees? That kind of thing?"

"Certainly."

"And the trust agreement? Who holds that? You?"

"The bank."

"Bert Clancy?"

"Bert is one of the trustees."

So? Johnny filed the information away in his mind to ask Bert about. He turned his thoughts to the notes he had brought from Saul Pentland's lab. "Did Harrington carry insurance?"

"He did indeed. A million-dollar policy on his life. An umbrella liability policy of five million. Plus, of course, homeowner's and automobile insurance, the usual things."

"And who," Johnny said, "is the beneficiary of the life policy?"

"His parents, Waldo and Lucille Harrington."

"So there it is," Johnny told Cassie that night. They were sitting in front of the fireplace where piñon logs, standing on end after the local custom, gave off their fragrance as they crackled and burned. "That's all we know, as of now."

As Johnny well knew, Cassie thought, on a dig, anthropologists divided the area into careful, rectangular units, marking the boundaries of each and giving each a number. Whatever was discovered in the ground was immediately tagged with the number of the area from which it had come, because in the end, the juxtaposition of the discovered articles could be even more important than most of the articles themselves in solving the larger questions of what kind of life had been lived here, and how it had been organized.

In his own way, Cassie had long ago discovered, Johnny worked in similar fashion, gathering his bits of information and opinion, labeling them, and keeping them separate in his mind until the time came to assemble them into a whole. "A fruitful day's work," she said.

"Lots of questions. Few answers."

"Which," Cassie said, "is exactly the way you like it, no?" Her smile seemed to fill the room. "And you already have hunches, no doubt." Her voice was soft

33

with understanding. "And your hunches frequently turn out to be right."

Here was the wonder, Johnny thought as he had thought so many times before, that she did understand him, and, more important, cared enough about him not to question his hunches, or try to pry into their rationale.

Always, until he had met this woman, he had been alone in the world, a *coyote,* a mixture, fitting into none of the three ethnic backgrounds that had produced him, carrying a chip on his shoulder for all to see, instantly ready to take offense or action against any slight, real or imagined, contemptuous of those who for whatever reasons had not clawed their way out of poverty or squalor as he had but had merely resigned themselves instead to complaining about a way of life no better and perhaps even worse than that which they had been born into.

Two misfits, he often thought, Cassie and himself, somehow finding in each other the kind of ease and comfort neither had ever expected to know. There was the miracle.

He produced one of his rare genuine smiles. "You," he said, "are something else, *chica."* Instantly the smile turned inward again, mocking himself. "You see, I'm even picking up current Anglo jargon. I'll be saying 'okay' and 'have a nice day' next."

He went out after dinner that night. "Possibly a pub crawl," he told Cassie. "Tony Lopez, who'd make a good gossip columnist, came up with a name, Harrington's current girl. Tony says she's best found at night."

His first stop was Sam's bar, where Sam herself came over to greet him. Sam was a big, strong, handsome woman, always a mine of information. "A drink?" Sam said. "On the house?"

Johnny shook his head, smiling. "Trying to seduce me?"

"That'll be the day." Sam's smile matched his own. "But if I cared at all about men, you'd be high on the list. As it is, you're safe." She studied his face. "You have that hunting look. Who is it this time?"

"Girl named Penny Lincoln. You know her?"

"This is about that bastard Charley Harrington? Level with me, *amigo.*"

Johnny merely nodded.

"Penny's a mixed-up kid," Sam said. She nodded to a lonely corner table. "Sitting right over there. What's she doing here? It's because she doesn't know what she is—goes both ways and feels real uptight about it." Sam studied Johnny's face. "Shocked? No, you wouldn't be. You're too smart for that. But maybe you don't know that AC-DC's a hell of a lot more common than most people think, so she isn't unique by a long shot. But most, a lot of them married women, just take it in stride and enjoy themselves."

"You're a philosopher, Sam."

"Nope. I've just come to terms with myself. Took you a long time too, didn't it? In a different way? You don't seem to hate the world the way you once did."

True, thanks to Cassie, but Johnny had not realized that it was quite so obvious. Or maybe it wasn't; Sam saw deep.

"That Cassie," Sam said, as if she had been reading his thoughts, "is quite a girl." She switched the subject with another nod in Penny Lincoln's direction. "You want an introduction?"

"I think I can manage," Johnny said.

Penny Lincoln looked up as he approached her table, pulled out a chair, and sat down. "Cop, aren't you?" she said.

Johnny nodded. Pretty girl, he thought, but without formed character in the regular features, the short-cut hair, the blue eyes that did not look quite straight at him. "Been expecting me?" he said.

"I suppose so." She sat up then, squared her shoulders, and thrust out full breasts clearly visible beneath her tank top. "Let's get on with it."

"For starters," Johnny said, and his voice was neither gentle nor belligerent, merely businesslike, "when did you see Harrington last?"

"Yesterday."

"About what time?"

The girl's voice was tight with either nervousness or resentment, or maybe both. "You want chapter and verse, right?"

"It would help."

"Who? You? Or me?"

"I think all of us."

The girl was silent for a few moments; from her deep breathing, Johnny thought, trying to steady herself. "Okay," she said. "We had lunch. At Ernie's." She glared defiantly. "You know Ernie's? It's—"

"I know Ernie's. A good restaurant."

"Yeah." The girl seemed to relax a little. "Not like those fast-food dumps. We took our time. I had wine, white wine, red's too strong. Charley had the same damn thing he always drank, vodka and cranberry juice. Tastes terrible, but he said it has vitamins or something. You want to know what we had to eat?"

"I don't think that's necessary. What time did you leave?"

"And where did we go and what did we do? What do you think?"

"Why don't you tell me?"

"Okay. It's no damn secret. We left maybe two o'clock in that wild Ferrari of his. We went to my studio and we went to bed. It took some time, the way it always did, the way he liked it. You want to know all about that?"

"I don't think I need details."

The girl took a deep, unsteady breath that made her breasts tremble against the tank top, nipples taut; perhaps, Johnny thought, with remembered passion. "Say what you want about Charley," she said, "but he was—well, never mind the details—he was some kind of stud."

"You were in love with him?" Johnny's voice was gentle.

"What the hell is love?" Shallow, juvenile cynicism was plain. "I liked him . . . enough, even though he was weird at times."

"How so?"

Penny spread her hands. She chewed her fingernails, Johnny noticed, and her hands were indifferently clean. "He just sometimes wasn't there," Penny said. "You know what I mean? Like right in the middle of—okay, screwing—he'd just go off somewhere, all by himself."

"You don't mean physically?"

"No." There was scorn in the denial. "What I mean is like he'd think of something all at once—you could tell from his eyes—and he'd go off like into a cloud or something where nobody else was."

Johnny had been told by someone, probably Cassie, that Goethe sometimes used to work out poetic rhythms with his fingers on his mistress's back during their lovemaking. "I think I understand," Johnny said.

Penny looked at him in sudden anger. "Look. Am I, like they say, a suspect? I don't know anything about shotguns and I'd be scared to death to shoot one. I don't say Charley was a nice guy because I guess he wasn't—all those stories about him—but I liked him, like I said, enough, and he never played rough the way some guys do, and he took me nice places and I liked riding in that wild car of his, and he was real good in bed. He knew what a girl likes and—" She stopped, and suddenly her eyes were filled with tears. "Damn it, why'd you come in here, anyway?"

"Just one more question," Johnny said. "What time did he leave your studio, and did you go with him?"

The girl ignored the tears that ran down the sides of her nose. "Hell, no," she said. "I was—pooped, you know, beat. I wasn't going anywhere."

"What time did he leave?"

Penny wiped her eyes with the backs of her hands. "It was getting dark. He'd already turned on the lights because he liked, you know, to see me and I liked it too. I don't know the goddamn time, maybe six, seven, something like that. I heard him blast off in that car of his, and then I, well, I went to sleep."

Johnny pushed back his chair and stood up. "Thanks, Penny."

There was no answer. He had expected none.

Sam stopped him on his way out. "Like I said, mixed-up, no?"

Johnny merely nodded.

"I feel sorry for her," Sam said, "and others like her. They don't wear flowers in their hair any more, or granny dresses and hiking boots, but they're the same spaced-out kids looking for God-knows-what, something they sure as hell didn't find at home."

"I know what you mean," Johnny said, and thought, there, in a way, but for the wonder of Cassie go I.

"Yes," Sam said, "I think you do. See you around, *amigo.*"

It was near midnight when Johnny let himself into the house. Cassie was already in bed, but Chico was waiting for him, tail aloft and waving. In the corner fireplace the dying embers of the piñon fire still threw out welcome heat. It was altogether, Johnny thought, a fine, warm scene to come home to. He pulled Chico's soft ears and spoke to him quietly. "Good boy," he said, and smiled to himself at the open ecstasy the sound of his voice produced as he went on into the bedroom, undressed in the dark, and slipped in beside Cassie's warmth.

"I'm awake," she said. "Did you find her?"

He recounted the scene and, remembering Sam's description, summed up with, "Lost and bewildered." And immediately added in surprise, "Listen to me, *chica,* feeling sorry for someone."

Cassie's hand touched his cheek gently. "You do have feelings, you know, just like people."

"I don't think I did—until I met you."

The touch became a gentle caress. "Shall I say, 'Likewise'?"

"Let's explore that," Johnny said, reaching for her. "Together."

4

Tony Lopez was waiting when Johnny came downtown in the morning. "The silly season is usually around fiesta time," Tony said, "but it seems to have come late this year. First, Harrington. Now another foul ball." He consulted a typed report. "Cathcart, Ross and wife, Grace." He looked at Johnny. "Mean anything?"

"Just a name."

"Commodities trader, big stuff. They've been two months fishing in Scotland and, quote, theater-going in London. Got home late yesterday. House torn apart. Housesitter missing, fellow named Glenn Ronson, ex-highway department equipment operator." Tony laid the report on Johnny's desk. "Joey Portilla went out to see them last night."

Johnny sat down. "Burglary?"

"Nothing missing, Cathcart says."

Johnny was frowning faintly. "So?"

"That's what he told Joey. Then he collapsed. He's in the coronary care unit at the hospital. Nobody's seen Ronson in some time, near as Joey could find out. Just—disappeared."

Johnny was still frowning. There was an undertone in Tony's voice speaking of something not yet revealed. "What aren't you saying?" he said.

Tony spread his big hands. "Maybe nothing. Like I said, half Santo Cristo County didn't like Charley Harrington."

"And Cathcart is one of that half?"

Tony took his time. "Cousin of mine used to clean for the Cathcarts. She said Cathcart raised all kinds of hell because he thought Charley Harrington had tapped his phone."

"Had he?"

Tony shrugged. "Phone company said no; at least they didn't think so. That made Cathcart even madder. He said he was going to get the little son of a bitch."

"Your cousin heard that?"

"She says."

Johnny leaned back in his chair and stared at the wall. "Interesting," he said. He missed Tony's expression which said clearly: Here we go again. "Nothing missing," Johnny went on, "but he collapsed from heart trouble. Why?" He did look up at Tony then, and produced one of his rare smiles. "Or am I just suspicious of everyone and everything?"

Tony consulted his notes again. "His doctor's name is Ashley, Richard Ashley, in case you were wondering. And Waldo Harrington is on his way here from the airport."

Waldo Harrington arrived within a matter of minutes, a small, slight man in his fifties, wearing a rumpled suit he had no doubt flown in all the way from Japan. He talked in quick phrases and sentences as if finding it difficult to make his words keep pace with his mind.

If Harrington had felt any grief upon hearing of his son's death, Johnny thought, he had come to terms with it and tucked it away out of sight. The long flight from Japan would have provided ample time for much thought about many things.

"I can't say I'm surprised, Lieutenant. That's not the right thing to say, I know, but there it is. Charley was, well, Charley, and there were times when it seemed to Lu and me that he spent his time just trying to make enemies. I don't know why. We're physicists, not psychiatrists, and *things, facts* are what we know, not people." He paused, his eyes on Johnny's face. "I'm sorry, but that's how it is." He paused again. "I guess that makes me a damn poor parent, and I'm sorry about that too. I've been sorry for a long time."

Johnny merely nodded. He pushed across his desk the notes from Harrington's pockets which contained mathematical symbols and equations. "Can you tell me anything about these?"

Waldo bent forward to study them. He was silent for a long time before he looked up and leaned back in his chair again. "Interesting," he said, "but I haven't the foggiest notion what they may apply to. If anything. Charley was a better mathematician than either of us, and we aren't all that bad." He smiled then for the first time, a somehow wistful smile. "By the time he was nine, he was beating me consistently at chess, completely out of my class. Those"—he indicated the notes—"could be just a sort of doodling. Or they could be pieces of something he was working on, maybe a theoretical problem he thought he'd finally found a way to whip. There's no way to know."

Johnny nodded again. His face and his voice were expressionless. "Can you tell me why he wanted to talk to you and Mrs.—Doctor—your wife about insurance?"

Waldo smiled again, in faint amusement this time. "We don't use the title *Doctor*, Lieutenant. That's reserved for physicians. At the lab a Ph.D. is more or less assumed. And the answer is no. I didn't even know he wanted to talk to us. He didn't very often these last few years." The smile had disappeared.

"He carried insurance," Johnny said.

"Did he?" Waldo was silent for only a moment, turning the matter over in his quick mind. "I never thought about it before, but of course he would. He was out in the world. I guess we tend to forget that. We're part of the lab, and there are people there who worry about things like insurance. We don't. I never thought much about that before, either. I guess we're rather insulated."

"His life was insured for a million dollars."

Waldo's lips pursed in a soundless whistle. "That's a great deal of money, Lieutenant. I mean for—people. It isn't much when you're talking about a project. But for one person?" He shook his head in bewilderment.

"You and your wife are the beneficiaries, Mr. Harrington. You didn't know that?"

Waldo took off his glasses, looked at them, and put them back on again.

It was, Johnny decided, an automatic gesture either

of total astonishment or deep emotion. Maybe both, he told himself, and said nothing.

Waldo said at last, "You wouldn't be pulling my leg, Lieutenant?" He studied Johnny's face carefully and then shook his head. "No," he said, "you're serious." He spread his hands. "I don't know what to say. Your question has clear implications. They follow logically. The answer is no, Lieutenant. I knew nothing about any insurance, and I am sure Lu is just as ignorant as I am." It was a faint, wry smile this time, quickly gone. "Proving a negative is always difficult, in mathematics or in theoretical physics—or in almost any other discipline I know. It is impossible here. You have only my statement that we knew nothing of any insurance, nothing at all."

"I think I believe you," Johnny said.

"But you have to check, of course. I understand."

Johnny was silent for a few moments. "Does the Charles Harrington Foundation mean anything to you, Mr. Harrington."

"I didn't even know there was such a thing."

"But you don't seem surprised."

Waldo Harrington shook his head slowly. "I'm afraid, Lieutenant," he said, "that you have already exhausted my capacity for surprise by the business of insurance. May I ask what the foundation is, or does?"

"We're both in the dark," Johnny said. "It hasn't been established, so I don't know either. Yet," he added.

Johnny sat for a long time just staring at the wall after Waldo Harrington had left. There was little more, if anything, to be found out in the parents' direction, he decided; they probably knew a great deal less about their son's activities than any number of other people. Still, it would be well to keep them in mind, if only loosely.

But right now, he decided, it would be best to find out as much as he possibly could about Charley Harrington's past. Since, as he had told Cassie, folks did not walk around carrying scatterguns, it was almost certain that the murder was planned rather than carried out on sudden impulse, so the motive would logically lie in the past.

Hold the phone, he told himself: Folks seldom walked around carrying scatterguns, true, but even when they kept them at home, and handy, they almost never had them loaded with double-ought buckshot. That was heavy stuff.

He called for Tony Lopez. "I doubt if many stores even carry double-ought loads. There'd be no call for them."

Tony nodded. It was, he told himself, something he ought to have seen for himself. "On my way," he said.

Johnny stood up. Now for some more background. From the source.

The Santo Cristo Juvenile Court was housed these days in the new judicial complex which, despite its newness, already smelled of municipal officialdom. The Honorable Eloy C. de Baca, longtime juvenile court judge, was in his chambers in his shirt-sleeves with a half-empty glass of diet cola on his desk.

"Irregular," he told Johnny, after hearing his request.

Johnny shrugged.

"The deceased was over twenty-one when he perished, Lieutenant. What you are asking for, then, are records that are at least three years old, and are by law confidential anyway."

"Entendido, understood," Johnny said.

The judge sipped his diet cola and set the glass down carefully. "Between us," he said in Spanish, "the deceased was a juvenile stinker of the first category. If someone had shot him or knifed him as a result of any one of a number of his performances, I wouldn't have been at all surprised. But that was three years ago, and as far as I know, he hasn't gone badly astray since." He switched abruptly to English. "You think the seeds might be in his record?"

"Es possible. But I won't have any way of knowing unless I know about the record."

The judge leaned back in his chair and stared reflectively at the ceiling. "Rape," he said, ticking off the points on his fingers, "attempted rape, vehicular violations by the handful, including one vehicular homicide, computer theft—you probably know about that one—attempted murder, vandalism—"

Johnny's eyebrows rose. "That seems out of place."

The judge nodded. "It did at the time. He was accused and charged, but I deemed the evidence insufficient and the charges were quashed."

"Who charged him?"

The judge frowned. "As I said, juvenile charges are by law confidential."

"I know."

"You know," the judge said, "and care neither a jot nor a tittle—I think those are the words I remember from somewhere." He shook his head, smiling faintly. "Perseverance is your trademark, isn't it? As I recall, the charges were brought by a man named Cathcart. He disliked the boy, which merely made him one of a

47

large majority. But, as I said, I deemed the evidence insufficient, although"—again he lapsed into Spanish —"between us, I am inclined to believe that young Harrington was guilty. The ingenuity of the alleged vandalism, having to do with altering the Cathcarts' telephone wiring, tended to indicate that it was no ordinary juvenile prank."

"Ross Cathcart?" Johnny said without inflection.

"I believe that was the name."

Well, well, Johnny thought, and wondered what was to be made of that. "And the vehicular homicide? Who was the victim?"

"An elderly man named Sanchez. Frank Sanchez, I believe it was. It could have been unavoidable on an unlighted street, and I chose to rule that it was."

Johnny tucked it away in his mind. "Only one more thing. You mentioned attempted murder."

The judge smiled faintly. "It was so claimed. If that was the actual intent, it was one of young Harrington's rare recorded failures. I found too much doubt to do other than dismiss the case."

Johnny sat silent, waiting.

"Perseverance," the judge said, *"and* patience. A formidable combination, Lieutenant." He switched again to Spanish. "One of Harrington's employees at his CH Company. Oh, yes, it was a going concern while Harrington was still a juvenile. The employee was almost electrocuted by a wire that was allegedly disconnected, but was not. Harrington was blamed, naturally. Harrington's reputation was such that he was blamed for almost anything that occurred while he was in the neighborhood."

"And the alleged victim?" Johnny said.

"I read in the paper that he had died of natural causes a year or so ago." The judge smiled benignly. "So unless the teachings of the Church are fallacious, which may God forbid, he could scarcely have been your murderer, Lieutenant."

Johnny stood up. *"Muchísima gracias."*

"Nada, nothing," the judge said, "and I mean literally. I have said nothing."

"Entendido, understood."

There was a note on Johnny's desk when he returned. "Ben Hart called. Call him." A telephone number was given which Johnny promptly dialed. There were not too many in Santo Cristo who, in Johnny's opinion, deserved instant attention. Ben Hart was one.

A pleasant, modulated female voice on the phone said, "Flora Hobbs speaking."

Johnny smiled into the phone. Flora was a friend from way back. "Johnny Ortiz, Flora. Ben's there?"

"Sipping on my bourbon. If you can picture Ben sipping. Here he is."

Ben's voice was as large and as hearty as the man himself. "Got a little problem, Johnny. Hold right still and I'll come down and tell you about it. That's me you see coming in the door."

Johnny hung up and leaned back in his chair to stare again at the wall. So Ross Cathcart had charged Charley Harrington with vandalism, presumably because of the alleged phone tap. So? Given what Johnny already knew of Charley Harrington, he could picture the *boy* working up to some kind of retaliation, but he failed to see how by any stretch of even his

49

imagination the incident could have led to Cathcart's deciding to take up a shotgun with murder in mind. Still, in due course, Cathcart deserved a little talk.

"Morning, boy!" Ben Hart filled the doorway.

Ben was a local rancher, as much a fixture in the Santo Cristo community, and the state, as the ancient Palace of the Governors on the plaza. He was approximately Saul Pentland's enormous size, and despite his years carried only a little excess weight. He was dressed in faded jeans hung low on his hips by a tooled leather belt with a silver-and-turquoise buckle, heeled boots, and a flannel shirt—cotton in summer, wool in late fall and winter—with the sleeves turned up on his massive forearms.

He sat down, filling the visitor's chair to capacity, and pushed his battered and sweat-stained hat back from his forehead, disclosing an area of white skin that contrasted strangely with the rest of his face. "One of my boys saw buzzards circling this morning and went out to see if maybe we'd lost a cow." He shook his head. "A man, what's left of him, about a mile inside my cattle guard on the highway entrance and fifty-sixty yards into the scrub growth. Been there a spell, looks like."

"You've called the state police?"

Ben shook his head. "State police and I sometimes butt heads a bit. They'd purely love to think I caught the fellow on my land and maybe gave him a little too good of a lesson about trespassing."

Nothing changed in Johnny's face. "Did you, Ben?"

"Nope. Any time I shoot a man, I do it head-on. That is, I used to. Haven't had occasion for a long time."

It was hard not to smile, Johnny thought, but there

was only fact behind Ben's words. The truth was that the old man meant exactly what he said. He went back far enough to remember when arguments were still sometimes settled by gunfire, and Ben had never been one to back down for anybody, or anything.

"One more thing," Ben said. "I never used a scattergun against a man in my life. Scatterguns are to shoot birds with."

Nothing changed in Johnny's face. He said slowly, "Scattergun, Ben? You're sure?"

"Hell's bells, I know what a load of buckshot can do, boy! Like I said, I never held with it, but I've seen it before and it's not pretty. Same thing as happened to that Harrington kid, isn't it?"

Johnny nodded.

"That's why I thought maybe you'd take over here," Ben said. "The state cops got books they read, and rules, and they think I'm as out of date as peep-sights and single-action handguns."

Johnny smiled. "Your place is out of my jurisdiction, Ben."

"Hell's bells, I know that."

"On the other hand," Johnny said, "I'll see what I can do." Use of a shotgun loaded with buckshot changed the entire situation.

Ben heaved himself out of the chair, which protested the sudden strain. "Appreciate it. If you want me, I'll be back up at Flora's. There's still some of that good whiskey left in my glass." He added as an afterthought, "I haven't let anybody move him. Just kept the buzzards and the skunks away." He walked out and down the hall with the rolling gait of the lifelong horseman.

Johnny called the state police and spoke briefly, and

without belligerence. In the end, satisfied, he hung up and called Doc Means.

"We've got another one, Doc. Out on Ben Hart's spread. This one apparently is shotgun too. The state people have given it to me. I'll send Tony Lopez out with you."

"Business," Doc said, "is brisk." And then, "I was going to call you. We figure Harrington had been dead maybe twelve, maybe twenty hours when the kids found him. That help?"

One more little piece, Johnny thought, one more direction to take; it all helped. The question was, how much?

Johnny saw Dr. Richard Ashley, the cardiologist attending Ross Cathcart, by appointment that afternoon. "Mr. Cathcart," the doctor said, "is coming along fine. We have rhythm restored, and his EKG looks normal." He was silent. "A healthy man, Mr. Cathcart. There seems to have been no warning."

"Heart attacks do happen without warning, don't they?"

The doctor leaned back in his chair. "This was not really, properly speaking, a heart attack. Arrhythmia is the better term, a lack of synchronization between the upper and lower chambers of the heart." He studied Johnny's face. "You follow me?"

"Assume I don't."

"Put simply," the doctor said, "the two upper chambers of the heart, the atria, receive the blood and pass it along, through valves, to the lower chambers, the ventricles, which are the pumps that push the blood through the body. Atrial fibrillations, such as

Mr. Cathcart had, are, in effect, muscular flutters of the upper chambers instead of rhythmic pulsations, and they may be as rapid as three hundred and fifty flutters a minute; whereas the lower chambers, the ventricles trying to receive the blood in order to pump it out, may be pulsing at eighty times a minute. Obviously the valves cannot cope with the discrepancy and the heart engine is no longer functioning properly."

"Life threatening?"

"Rarely. We have ways of restoring the rhythm, and since there is rarely heart damage, normal function is also restored. But the patient is left feeling weak, since during the fibrillations, the body's blood supply has been less than normal." The doctor smiled. "One of my patients told me that during fibrillations, one has intimations of mortality, which I suppose is as good a way as any to describe the feelings that seem to come with any noticeable alteration in the heart's performance."

Johnny said, "And what can cause these fibrillations?"

The doctor spread his hands. "Impossible to say, except that many, and perhaps most, sudden heart problems are somehow stress related."

Johnny thought about it and then stood up. "Thanks. I can see Cathcart, talk to him? Or is he still in the coronary care unit?"

"He's resting comfortably in a private room. No problem about seeing him."

Cathcart, in fresh pajamas, cordovan slippers, and a silk robe, was sitting in the hospital room's one easy chair, reading a financial magazine. He glanced at

53

Johnny's identification with distaste. "I believe I have already told the police all I know, Lieutenant," he said.

Johnny sat on a straight chair. "Maybe you'll tell me part of it again. Glenn Ronson—had he house-sat for you before?"

"A number of times. He is retired from the highway department, and we pay him a small monthly fee to keep himself available to sit for us. But if you will bother to read the report, Lieutenant, you will see that I declared nothing missing from the house."

"Except Glenn Ronson, which is a fairly important exception."

"His disappearance has nothing to do with me. We were overseas."

"All right," Johnny said, "we'll put him aside for a moment." And then, a sudden wild thought. "I may even know where he is, but no matter. Doesn't it strike you as strange that somebody would ransack a house the size of yours, obviously containing valuables, and not take anything?"

"I do not pretend to understand the criminal mind, Lieutenant."

"Unless, of course," Johnny said as if Cathcart had not spoken, "he was looking for something specific and didn't find it." He looked straight at Cathcart then, unsmiling. "What do you suppose that might be?"

"I have no idea, Lieutenant, none at all. I'm afraid I can't be of any help. Mrs. Cathcart is understandably upset, as I am—"

"Nothing taken," Johnny said. "Nothing destroyed." He was still looking straight at Cathcart.

"Lieutenant," Cathcart said, "I have been through

a rather harrowing physical experience. It has left me very tired. Unless you have something other than wild speculation to discuss—" He left the sentence unfinished.

Johnny stood up. *"Bueno,"* he said, "we'll postpone any further talk." He reached the door, stopped and turned. "You're a commodities trader, aren't you?"

"And precisely what does that have to do with anything?"

"I don't know," Johnny said, and added, "yet." He nodded then. "Get well," he said, and walked out.

5

Tony Lopez was back. "I've got Patsy Valdez phoning stores about double-ought buckshot. She's runner-up just about every year in the state trapshoot, so she knows what she's asking about." He paused long enough to watch Johnny's approving nod. "And Doc and Saul and I all went out to Ben Hart's place." He shook his head. "Bad," he said. "Worse than Harrington. Been dead, Doc thinks, maybe a week, ten days, but that's just a fast guess."

Johnny nodded again.

"Identifying him is going to take some doing. Doc and Saul are getting on it."

"Ben Hart said fifty-sixty yards from the driveway," Johnny said. *Driveway* was something of a misnomer; the graded drive from the cattleguard to Ben's big house was something over eight miles. "How'd he get there? Walk? Tracks?"

"Not with the rains we had last week. Not even you could figure that one out. And both Doc and Saul are sure he wasn't killed there. Harrington all over again."

"Bueno." Johnny thought about the leap of imagination that had come to him while he was talking to Cathcart. Wild, but possible, he thought. "Tell Doc and Saul to bear in mind that it just might be old Glenn Ronson, the Cathcarts' house-sitter," he said.

Tony Lopez pursed his lips and whistled softly. "You're hearing voices? *Madre de Dios,* what's the connection?"

"I don't know." Simple truth.

Tony rolled his eyes and shook his head wonderingly. Then he sighed. *"Bueno.* I'll tell them."

"Cathcart," Johnny said, switching the subject, "brought a charge of vandalism against Harrington for tapping his phone. Why was he so uptight? Nobody wants a tap on his line, but this seems like overreaction."

Tony nodded. "I asked my *prima* and she said Cathcart claimed Harrington was listening to his orders to his broker to buy or sell, which didn't make much sense, just a kid listening—"

"But the kid was Charley Harrington," Johnny said and nodded yet again. *"Bueno.* There might be something in that. Or maybe—" He stopped and stared at the wall.

Tony watched and waited. No telling what might come out, he thought. From time to time he found himself conjuring up pictures of Johnny squatting on his heels, possibly wearing only a breechcloth, staring into the smoke of a tiny fire, seeing visions invisible to ordinary folks. Johnny had that look on his face now. Tony was tempted to cross himself.

"There might even be more to it than that," Johnny said at last, and shook his head with finality. *"Basta! That can wait.* Now, an elderly man named Sanchez, Frank Sanchez—"

"Killed by a car a few years back. Some juvenile, so no names came out." He frowned at Johnny. "Harrington?"

"Off the record, yes. Who was Sanchez?"

Tony blew his breath out in a long sigh. "Related to half of Santo Cristo, maybe more than that. Frank was, well, Frank. *Simpático.* Liked kids. Nothing special. Worked as a bank guard and then did something for the county, or maybe it was the other way around." He spread his hands. "Fiesta once, he bought me a *burrito.* I'm not sure, but I think he thought I was one of his grandsons. He had them by the dozens."

"No connection with Harrington?"

Tony thought about it and shook his head. "None I can see. Frank was strictly *chicano,* if you see what I mean. Oh, he knew Anglos, sure. You can't live in Santo Cristo without running into lots of them. But Frank didn't speak very good English and hadn't gone much to school and he liked his own friends and family, you know, people he was comfortable with. He would have been real uncomfortable with a firecracker like Harrington even if he was just a kid."

Johnny said, "Bank guard. Which bank?"

"The right one." Tony nodded. "But even there it doesn't add up. Frank's job was seeing to it that people not on bank business didn't park in the lot, and that the little drawers for deposit slips and things like that were kept filled, that kind of thing. He wouldn't have known a computer if he'd met one."

"Bueno." Johnny produced his faint smile. "You've convinced me. Maybe accidental manslaughter, but almost certainly nothing more." You narrowed the list when and as you could; progress in a negative kind of way.

The phone on Johnny's desk rang. Saul Pentland's deep voice said, "One of these days you're going to run out of hunches, but they're still working for you now. There *were* traces of blood in that passageway, on the tiles and on the walls. I couldn't testify to it in court, but it's a very good bet that Charley Harrington was blasted, like you said, when he came in from the garage. We found blood traces on the door too. Type O. Charley's."

Johnny said, "Thanks," and hung up to look again at Tony Lopez. "So now we know where Harrington was killed, and about when. All we need is why and who."

Tony snapped his fingers with the sound of a pistol shot. "Like I said, little things like that."

"One more thing," Johnny said. "If it turns out that the dead man on Ben's property *is* Glenn Ronson, see if he was carrying any keys." A new line of thought was beginning to take shape.

"Everybody carries keys," Tony said.

"But find out anyway. And where he lived when he wasn't house-sitting. Did he live alone? Pension? Social Security? Known habits? Friends?"

"Todo?"

"Exactly."

"I like knifings better," Tony said. "They're more personal." He walked out.

Johnny looked up the number of Bert Clancy's bank, and called. Clancy was in. "Charley Harrington set up a trust," Johnny said. "With your bank? Isn't that how these things usually work?"

"We executed a trust agreement with him," Clancy said. It was his banker's voice, cautious in tone.

"What does it take for me to find out what it says? A court order?"

There was hesitation. "Oh, hell," Bert Clancy said at last, "that's not necessary. It was an *inter vivo* trust, revocable at either Charley's or our option while he was alive, becoming irrevocable upon his death."

"The bank is trustee?"

"One of them. There are several."

"Do you want to name names?"

Again there was hesitation. "Between us, huh?"

"For now. If it all has to come out, I'll get a court order."

"Well," Bert Clancy said, "Waldo and Lucille Harrington are named. Then there's—"

"Wait a minute. Do they know they're named as trustees? Waldo and Lucille, I mean?"

"Why, I assumed so." There was a pause. "Although, come to think of it, maybe they don't, the way the trust agreement is set up. They are to be appointed trustees, if they so consent, only if and when the trust becomes irrevocable. That is, when Charley dies. So it wasn't considered necessary to get their signatures on the agreement."

"I'm no lawyer," Johnny said, "but isn't that unusual?"

"Hell's fire, everything Charley Harrington did was unusual. But that was the way he wanted it, and it was his money—more of it than I'll ever see."

"Bueno," Johnny said. "The bank, Waldo and Lucille Harrington—anybody else?"

"Joe Whitney, the lawyer."

"And that's it?"

"That's the list."

Johnny thought about it. "And the trust agreement sets up the Charles Harrington Foundation. Joe Whitney told me that."

"That's right."

"And what is the foundation supposed to do?"

"Give money away. For worthy causes. Like the Rockefeller and the Ford and the Carnegie and all the others."

Johnny went back to staring at the wall after he hung up. He was still at it when Tony Lopez appeared again in the doorway. Johnny ignored him for a few moments while he thought things through. Then, "Why does a man expect his parents to outlive him?" he asked, looking up. "Answer me that."

First we get hunches, Tony thought, now we get riddles. He said, "He doesn't expect to live very long." He hesitated. "Maybe he's got some disease, or—" He hesitated.

"Or what?"

Tony shrugged. "Maybe he thinks somebody's going to kill him." He studied Johnny's face. It showed nothing. "Are we talking about Charley Harrington?"

"We are."

"I was afraid of that," Tony said, and was silent, waiting.

"Bueno," Johnny said after a little time. "What have we got?"

Tony sighed. "Doc says to tell you you're a second-sighted heathen. It *was* Ronson. They went back and found a Social Security card and a driver's license in a wallet tossed off in the brush. Found that by accident. Prints on file because he was once a security guard with a handgun license." Tony shook his head at the wonder of it. "And he wasn't carrying any keys." He watched Johnny's eyebrows rise. "What makes that so important?"

"He was house-sitting, wasn't he?"

"Oh."

"And presumably he'd have had a key to get back into the house when he went out, no?"

Plain as the nose on your face, Tony told himself in disgust, only he hadn't seen it. *Estúpido!*

Lucille Harrington arrived home from the Washington congressional scene via the airport down in the city sixty miles away where she had left her car in the free-shuttle parking lot. She was a well-dressed and strikingly attractive woman who had kept her figure: in heels a trifle taller than Waldo, with short, graying hair, steady eyes of very bright blue, and an air of calm competence which very little could disturb.

She carried her own bag into their hillside home with its splendid views of the major mountains behind the city and found Waldo in his study just sitting and staring at the wall behind his desk. They kissed in a perfunctory way, and Lucille sat down in the leather visitor's chair.

"How was Washington?" Waldo said.

There was a flash of amusement in Lucille's blue eyes. "It was, as expected, hot, even in October, and filled with congressmen asking not very bright questions. How was Japan?"

"Crowded. 'Guchi sent his best."

Lucille nodded, acknowledging the greeting. "Now," she said, "preliminaries over. You saw the police lieutenant—Ortiz is his name?—and you are uncomfortable about it? Why?"

"Charley carried a life insurance policy in the amount of one million dollars. You and I are the beneficiaries."

Lucille thought about it briefly. "And what makes you uncomfortable—the amount of money, or the implications?"

"Very little disturbs you, does it, Lu?"

"The loss of a son disturbs me. But I won't wave my grief in public."

"You still think," Waldo said, "that he might one day have grown out of his ways?"

"And you don't?"

"No," Waldo said, "I don't. But then I didn't carry him in my body for nine months, and I appreciate the difference that may make."

Lucille said, "He could have been—" She stopped there, and was silent.

"Yes. He could have been one of the great ones. No argument. He chose his own directions instead."

"To impress us. To get out from under our shadow."

"Our fault then? You never said that before."

Lucille's face softened. "No fault," she said gently. "If he hadn't been what he was, he wouldn't have tried so hard to go his own way, to impress us with his abilities." She smiled without humor. "We were already impressed, but he didn't think that was enough." She closed her eyes briefly, and when she opened them again the air of calm competence had returned. "Does the policeman think we had something to do with his death? For the insurance?"

"He says not." Waldo was silent for a few moments. "You haven't met him, Lu. He is at least part Indian, Apache at a guess. And when he looks at you, you understand why the mere word Apache used to strike terror here in the Southwest."

"I'll talk to him," Lucille said. "And then I think we ought to set about showing him that we knew nothing about it."

Waldo smiled faintly as he had in Johnny's office. "How do you prove this negative?"

"By proving the positive, finding who was responsible."

"Playing detective?" Waldo shook his head. "Come off it, Lu."

"We have made our careers," Lucille said, "by applying logic to problems that needed to be solved. And I think we can say that we have done it rather well."

Waldo took off his glasses, looked at them, and put them back on again. Johnny had been right; the gesture indicated deep emotion. He shook his head slowly, in wonderment. "It is always astonishing to me, Lu," he said, "and even a little frightening when that adamantine side of you shows. You make up your mind, and nothing on earth will change it."

Lucille stood up. "It's been a long day, a boring flight, and the customary plastic airline lunch. I am tired, and hungry, and thirsty. Will you mix the martinis?"

Again that night after dinner, sitting with Cassie companionably close on the sofa, Chico at their feet with his chin on the toe of Cassie's boot, Johnny recounted the day's developments. It was an exercise almost of mental regurgitation, bringing out into the open within this intimate privacy and without careful editing, the facts, guesses, suppositions, doubts, and puzzlements that had accumulated within the last twenty-four hours. As always, the mere process was as soothing as a session in a steam bath.

Cassie listened quietly, staring at the fire as if its changing patterns produced a kind of hypnotic spell within which confusion rearranged itself into some kind of order. "Ross Cathcart," she said when Johnny was done.

"You know him, *chica?*"

"I've met him. Twice, no, three times. Once in Mexico City and twice in Guadalajara." She smiled without amusement, remembering. "Each time he bought me a drink and ended by inviting me to spend the night in his hotel room. I declined with appropriate thanks." She turned the suddenly amused smile on Johnny.

"Hijo de puta," Johnny said.

Cassie's smile spread. "Are you criticizing his taste?"

Johnny opened his mouth and closed it again. His expression softened and he too could smile. "Hardly. I'll have to give him that. He has an eye."

"Grace Cathcart," Cassie said, "is on the museum

board. He chose her with care too. She is a stunner with a taste for diamonds."

"I gathered that he was well-heeled."

"It isn't widely known," Cassie said, "although I don't think it's any secret that Ross Cathcart owns Johnson Gallery. His taste shows there too, especially in the sculptures, mostly bronzes that they handle." She was almost laughing now. "There is a female nude I think you would appreciate."

Johnny's smile was suddenly gone, and the harsh Indian lines of his features showed plain. "There was another female nude sculpture I remember. It was lovely. Until somebody cut its head off with a hacksaw."

Cassie shivered. "I remember. I haven't posed since. I don't think I could." She touched his arm with a gentle hand. "I led you away from your thoughts. Sorry."

Johnny was staring at the fire now. He shook his head slowly. "Maybe not. Cathcart interests me. Things happen to him. A kid, Harrington, taps his phone. His house-sitter gets himself killed." He turned to look at Cassie. "No connection, but—"

"But your antennae are beginning to quiver."

Johnny was silent, again staring at the fire, the dancing flames. Abruptly he stood up. "A little walk in the night, *chica*. I won't be long." He crossed the room in his light, soft-footed way, opened the door, and walked out without a backward glance.

Cassie watched the door close. She was smiling as she bent down to pull the dog's soft ears. "Thinking time, Chico. And he does it best outside, and alone." She felt no resentment, only deep understanding.

Outside the sky was black and the infinity of stars shone like tiny spotlights in their esoteric patterns. The scent in the air was of piñon and juniper, flavored by smoke from the chimney. Johnny drank it all in and felt refreshed.

He walked slowly, without conscious direction, his feet automatically finding, feeling, and adjusting to the contours of the ground, the softness of the dropped pine needles, the occasional rocks and outcroppings. What he experienced as he walked was not a cognitive process, but, rather, a kind of relaxation of mental control, allowing thoughts to come and go, to bubble up out of the hidden depths, to dissipate into nothingness and as suddenly return, sometimes augmented. He was alone in the night, and totally at ease. . . .

Cassie was still on the sofa reading a magazine when he returned. She carefully marked her place, put the magazine down, and sat quietly, waiting as he seated himself beside her.

"Maybe silly questions, *chica,*" Johnny said, "but I have to have them answered. Why did Charley Harrington tap Cathcart's phone in the first place? Was the tap ever removed, or was it so well-hidden that it was never really found? The phone company said they *thought* the line was tapped, and that implies that they weren't really sure." He looked at Cassie's face, her eyes. "Yes?"

Cassie nodded. "Follow your hunches. It is always best."

"The next question," Johnny said, "is why was Cathcart so upset when he merely suspected his line was tapped? Because a kid, even Charley Harrington, had been able to listen to orders to his broker?" He shook his head. "I won't buy it. Cathcart's a smooth customer. I don't think he upsets easily."

"And yet," Cassie said, "when he came home—"

"Good girl." Johnny was smiling. "That's the last question. Why the atrial fibrillations when nothing was missing? I won't buy that, either."

Cassie studied him. She began to smile. "You are wearing your scalping-knife look. It's that serious?"

"I want to know about Cathcart. And old Glenn Ronson, the house-sitter. And—"

"And the Harrington Trust? Is it still important?"

"All of it, *chica,* all of it. We're just beginning."

6

Ross Cathcart was discharged from the hospital on Thursday morning, three days after his overnight stay in the coronary care unit. His wife, Grace, came for him in her Jaguar, dressed in a tan silk shirt of price, tailored frontier trousers, and hand-crafted ostrich-skin cowboy boots, the costume finished off with small diamond earrings and her inevitable diamond finger rings, both engagement and wedding.

She was blond, tall, slim, and shapely. She rarely smiled. "Dick Ashley called," she told Cathcart after they were settled in the car and moving smoothly down the hospital drive. "He said no special care was required, but that you should be kept quiet for a few days."

"I have to go down to Mexico City."

Grace's eyebrows lifted slightly. "Why? We're just home."

69

"You're not interested in business," Cathcart said, "only in the money it brings. So let's just say I have matters to attend to. Okay?"

"If you say so." And, with no change of matter-of-fact tone, "The house is fairly well back in order. I can't see that anything is missing. The insurance broker called to ask, and—"

"When we have a claim, I'll let him know. Until then, it's none of his business. I'll call him and tell him that."

"You have a chip on your shoulder. Why?"

"I didn't enjoy the hospital experience. Or the reason for it."

Grace Cathcart did not take her eyes from the road. "What *was* the reason? I've been wondering."

"Where was that damned Ronson? Why wasn't he looking after things? He's not supposed to be a drunk, but—"

"He is dead. Killed by a shotgun, apparently just as the Harrington boy was." Still she kept her eyes straight forward. "Does that have significance, or—"

"Just what is that supposed to mean?"

"—is it just coincidence?" Grace Cathcart finished the question smoothly.

"How in hell would I know?"

"I couldn't say. I rarely understand what you know. Would you like lunch at home, or should we stop at Ernie's?"

"Home. I want a good, stiff drink. And some quiet."

Lucille Harrington called upon Johnny that same morning, and Johnny was more impressed than he would have cared to admit. She shook hands, sat down, crossed her ankles, and, with hands folded quietly in her lap, studied Johnny carefully and without embarrassment with those disconcertingly blue eyes for some moments before she spoke.

"My husband found you formidable, Lieutenant," she said in her own time. "I believe I agree with his assessment. And our position as the apparent beneficiaries of our son's insurance does not put us in a very favorable light. I quite understand that too."

It passed through Johnny's mind that there would be few things Lucille Harrington would not understand if she put her mind to them. He decided that silence was his best response.

"Does it follow then, Lieutenant, that if we choose to look into Charley's affairs that too will be regarded with suspicion?"

Johnny thought about it. "What kind of affairs?"

"Not his—peccadillos," Lucille Harrington said. "I am well-acquainted with those. Over the years they occupied a fair amount of my time."

Johnny could not resist saying, "He was a good boy?" A low blow, he thought, but he wanted to test reaction. He got the honesty he had expected.

"He was not a good boy, Lieutenant, as you must well know. In his rather unusual way he was a rather thorough scoundrel. Both my husband and I were quite aware of it. I don't want to labor the point, but there are various types of underprivilege in children. There are the deprived and the physically or mentally handicapped; those are obvious. There are also the exceedingly gifted who do not fit in with their peers, and there are those who grow up in what they see as the shadow of their parents—and rebel."

"And Charley was a combination of the last two."

"Astute of you, Lieutenant. Yes. That is not excuse for his actions; there is no excuse. Nor is there any excuse for our being unable to control him. We bear that blame."

"I understand."

"Yes," Lucille Harrington said, "I think you do. And I appreciate it. But to return to my original question: If we choose to investigate Charley's life after he left our home, will you find that suspicious? Or will you object?"

It was obvious that she was not finished, so Johnny remained silent.

"We have two reasons," Lucille said. "First, he *was* our son and it seems evident that he was murdered. We should very much like to know why and by whom, and see that something is done about it. I am not implying that you might feel otherwise."

Johnny restrained a smile, and nodded, acknowledging the point.

"Our second reason, Lieutenant, is to remove all doubts about our possible . . . complicity in his death."

Johnny nodded again. "Understood."

"We know very little about such matters," Lucille said. "In the crime novels I read on airplanes, in airport waiting rooms, and in hotel rooms the authorities are almost inevitably resentful of amateur . . . interference."

Johnny could smile openly then. "I wouldn't know—" And he hesitated, in his mind fumbling for a proper title of address.

The blue eyes saw and the quick mind immediately

understood his problem. *"Lucille* will do admirably, Lieutenant. Or Mrs. Harrington if you prefer formality. My husband probably told you that we do not use academic titles. Between us, we have a number, but they are only trotted out on solemn academic occasions along with the robes and the silly, archaic hats."

This was either the smartest woman he had ever encountered, Johnny was thinking, or she was totally and honestly without pretense, and probably both. However it was, his respect and admiration were growing rapidly. He said, "You probably have some directions in mind to investigate?"

During the entire conversation the hands folded quietly in her lap had remained totally immobile. She lifted and spread them now. They were strong and capable, with long fingers and short, shapely, carefully tended, buffed but not colored nails. "It would be pointless to cover ground you have already scrutinized," Lucille Harrington said. "Your reputation is that you do not miss very much. Oh, yes, we have been at some pains to find out what we could about you, Lieutenant. Research is our business, and we are reasonably proficient at it. No, I have suggested, and Waldo agrees, that the matter of Charley's finances and financial dealings might be worth looking into. Unless you have already preempted that field?"

For the first time, Johnny could lean back in his chair in total relaxation. And his rare smile reappeared. "Finances," he said, "are out of my line. If you and your husband want to poke around in those mysteries, I couldn't be happier."

Lucille Harrington stood up then. Her movements were both economical and graceful. She held out her hand. "I believe that we are going to get along quite well, Lieutenant—or may I call you Johnny?"

Johnny held out his hand. Her grip was solid, friendly. "Lucille," he said.

Lucille Harrington smiled. "Waldo and I will be in touch."

Johnny watched her walk down the hallway, erect, mature, distinctly feminine, but with the air of assured competence he normally associated with men. Cassie, he thought now, would smile at the concept, nod, make passing mention of male chauvinism, and then, in almost the same breath, point out that given the built-in bias of Johnny's early formative years, that tendency was probably inevitable.

Tony Lopez walked in to lean against the wall. "Much woman, *amigo*. Also much in here." He tapped his temple with his forefinger. "I don't think I could ever be sure what she's thinking."

A shrewd observation, Johnny thought, one to be kept in mind. He said, "Anything on Glenn Ronson?"

Tony consulted his notebook. "Highway department pension. Lived alone. His wife died years ago. No children. No police record. Has been house-sitting for the Cathcarts for four years whenever they travel, which is quite a bit of the time."

"You know about the Johnson art gallery? That Cathcart owns it?"

Tony nodded. "High-priced stuff. They don't carry much local talent, which doesn't make it very popular in the art set. Mostly name artists from the East or from Mexico. Cathcart's big on Mexico. Speaks good Spanish, *castellano.*"

Johnny thought about it. "The way I understand it,"

he said, "most commodity traders stick close in touch with the market one way or another. Way I hear it, you can lose your shirt while you take time out for the toilet. Does that figure with a lot of travel?"

Tony produced his look of resignation. "I have a cousin who is a stockbroker. I'll see what he can find out."

Congressman Mark Hawley flew home from Washington for the weekend. His first stop in town was Flora Hobbs's house for a drink of her good bourbon and a quick rundown on local doings.

Flora's house was known throughout the Southwest. Mere mention of it in male company brought smiles and understanding nods, and although various attempts had been made by civic-minded and other groups to have it shut down, it continued to exist as one of Santo Cristo's landmarks.

Flora was a widow from the East, in her sixties, slim, intelligent, educated, attractive, not at all the stereotypical madam. She allowed no scandal and no disturbances, and the social behavior of her girls was beyond reproach.

The house itself was one-story adobe, old, thick-walled, cool in summer, warm in winter, built around a central patio in which a fountain splashed and healthy cactus plants, cholla, prickly pear, hedgehog, pincushion, and claret cup, were scattered tastefully among lichen-covered volcanic rocks within carefully raked and weeded pea-gravel areas.

Congressman Hawley kissed Flora's cheek, settled himself in one of her leather visitor's chairs, accepted the proffered cut-glass decanter of bourbon and a glass, and sighed deeply. "Always good to get home again," he said. "I'm getting old, Flora. Slowing down."

"That will be the day." She smiled fondly. "Been a busy week, Mark. You've heard rumors?"

He nodded. "Now I want the whole story." He sipped his bourbon and listened quietly, and when she was done, "Probably could have predicted Charley Harrington would get it sooner or later. But Glenn Ronson?" The congressman shook his head. "Never hurt a fly. And why dump him on Ben's spread? Trying to point a finger? Won't work. Ben wouldn't use a scattergun. A rifle, more likely, or at close range a handgun."

Flora smiled. "So he said. Emphatically. From that chair."

Mark Hawley was holding his glass up to the light and admiring the whiskey's color. "Ross Cathcart," he said, dwelling thoughtfully on the name. "Maybe I better talk to Johnny Ortiz." He was silent again for a few moments. "But not down at police headquarters. Too many ears. Will you ask him up here, Flora, where we can talk in private? I'd appreciate it, almost as much as I appreciate this good whiskey."

And so Johnny, wanting mild exercise in the open air, walked up the hill to Flora's house, let himself in through the wrought-iron gate set in the adobe wall, and admired the cactus-planted entrance garden which complemented the patio as he walked up to the massive front door and banged the ancient iron knocker.

Flora left the congressman and Johnny alone in her study, the door closed. The congressman was a poker player from childhood, and he opened with caution as always. "You seem to have a fair helping on your plate, son. Any of it making any sense?"

Johnny shrugged. The old man would get around to what was on his mind in his own time, he thought, and he could afford to wait indefinitely with that built-in patience that came from his mother's people.

The congressman sipped his whiskey. "In the little time he was on the scene," he said, "Charley Harrington stirred up quite a bit of dust, wouldn't you say?"

"Quite a bit." Johnny's face and voice were expressionless.

"Funny thing about some people," the congressman said, "maybe most. There's usually a side of them that doesn't show much, maybe not at all. You've noticed that?"

"Now and again, yes."

The congressman poured himself more whiskey, and changed the subject. "Washington's a funny place. Most of the time it seems that damned little, if anything, ever happens, all those speeches and finagling, deals made here and compromises there, and you scratch the other fellow's back and he'll scratch yours, that kind of thing. With all that going on, it does look like the whole town just has its tail in its mouth and rolls around like a hoop never getting anywhere or amounting to much of anything." Talking was thirsty work. The congressman had another sip of whiskey. Neither in his voice nor in his manner was there any indication that the liquor was having an effect.

Johnny sat immobile, attentive. They were getting

near the meat of the matter, he told himself, and waited for a clue.

"But," the congressman said, "when you get right down to it, that town is still the heart, if not the soul, of this country. It's where the real power is, because power is knowing things and being able to find out the things you don't know, and the handles are right there, if you know where and how to pull them, to get just about anything you want laid out on the table to look at. I won't say it's fair, or even the way it ought to be, but that's the way it is." He smiled suddenly. "You going to ask me what I'm working up to?" He shook his head, answering his own question. "No. That's not your way. You'll just wait for me to come out with it."

"I'm in no hurry," Johnny said. Simple truth.

The congressman's smile resembled that of a crocodile in the shallows. "Times I wonder," he said, "just how in hell we Anglos ever managed to come out on top when we tangled with you savages."

"You stole our sheep."

"For a fact," the congressman said, and set his glass down. "All right. Charley Harrington wasn't what you might call a friend of mine. And he wasn't what you'd call a public-spirited citizen either. But like I said earlier, he had a side to him that didn't show and maybe I was about the only one he let get a look at it. It embarrassed him, but when he had his mind made up, he just went straight ahead and never looked back. Most single-minded character I ever did know, and I've known some ring-tailed wonders."

Johnny was wondering if he was beginning to see it

now, but he wanted it spelled out, and he sat, immobile and expressionless still, waiting patiently.

"I won't say Charley's motives were simon-pure," the congressman said. "It doesn't matter a damn whether they were or not. There was this fellow he didn't like much. I never knew why, and never asked. It was there, and it was plain, and it gave sense to Charley's reasons for coming to me. His basic reason, that was. There was another, and it was important too. Charley couldn't stand killing. Did you know that, son? He killed a man himself once."

Johnny nodded almost imperceptibly. Frank Sanchez, he was thinking.

"And," the congressman said, "it kind of broke him up, but he didn't let it show. And he *tried* to kill another man, did you know that? Well, he did, and between the two of them, he was finished with killing, any kind of killing. He wouldn't even shoot a gopher that was digging up his yard." The congressman smiled, remembering. "That was quite a talk we had over dinner one night in Washington. He let me see things I don't think he ever showed anybody else. Along with telling me what he knew about this fellow he didn't like. You know who it was?"

"Ross Cathcart." It had to be.

The congressman leaned back in his chair and studied Johnny's face, while his hand automatically found the glass and raised it to his lips. He savored his sip and lowered the glass again. His eyes had not left Johnny's. "You have a way of fooling me, son. This isn't the first time. You know things about Cathcart,

79

or are you just putting two and two together and coming up with five?"

"Just addition. And a little guesswork."

The congressman thought about it. Slowly he nodded. "Good. Let's leave it that way." He studied Johnny's face again. "You don't like that?"

"Not if it means I forget about Cathcart."

"That's pretty much what it means."

Johnny shook his head. All at once the harsh Indian features showed plain. "Somebody's going around killing people with a scattergun. Here in my town. Every time I look around, I see Cathcart. He—"

"The way I hear it," the congressman said, "Cathcart wasn't even in the country when Glenn Ronson was killed, and wasn't here in Santo Cristo when somebody gunned down Charley Harrington."

"Cathcart says. Maybe yes, maybe no. But he's in it somewhere, and I want to know where, and how, before I'll be satisfied."

There was a silence. "We've always gotten along, and I'd hate for us to butt heads, son," the congressman said.

"That's up to you."

"Suppose I said that important matters are involved? And it'll be best if they don't get tangled up by folks poking around?"

Johnny shook his head again. "Like you said, all those speeches and finagling, yes, and flag-waving coming out of Washington." His smile too was harsh. "Talk about treaties too, when it suits them, come to that. And then you steal our sheep—"

"Long time ago, son."

"Has anything changed?"

The congressman sighed, picked up his glass, looked at it, and set it down again. "I'm sorry you feel that way," he said. "Maybe I don't blame you much, all things considered. But I'm still sorry."

Johnny stood up. "Was that all?"

"For now, son. For now."

7

Charley Harrington's body was cremated and his ashes scattered on the hillside beneath his house. As stipulated in his will, there was no service of any kind.

His safe-deposit box at the bank was opened by Joseph Whitney, his lawyer, in the presence of a representative of the State Department of Taxation and Revenue. In it were the deed of trust for Charley's house and land, the deeds for his two automobiles, his birth certificate, a passport which had never been used, his life insurance and umbrella liability policies, and a sealed envelope with Charley's signature across the flap and the names of his parents on the front.

The tax man held it up to the light. "Near as I can tell, it's just a letter. But just to be sure it isn't bearer bonds or something like that—"

"Nonsense," Whitney said. "Just as you said, a letter to his parents. I'll deliver it."

"Fine," the tax man said. "I'll go along with you."

Whitney opened his mouth and closed it again carefully. "Suit yourself," he said.

Lucille Harrington accepted the envelope, looked without expression at Charley's scrawled signature, and then with an ivory letter opener, a gift from a Chinese physicist, slit it open. She opened the enclosed typed sheets, exposed their faces briefly to the tax man, and then refolded them. "A personal letter," she said, "as you can see." Her voice was quiet and steady, and her face showed no emotion.

"Yes, ma'am. Thank you," the tax man said, and went out to his car.

Lucille Harrington looked at Whitney. "Thank you for bringing it," she said. "Now if you will excuse us—"

Whitney said, "There are matters concerning—"

"Later," Lucille Harrington said in a tone that admitted no further discussion.

Together she and Waldo saw Whitney out, and when the door was closed, Lucille leaned back against it and faced her husband. "I don't remember when last I cried," she said as two large tears rolled unheeded down the sides of her nose. Her voice was no longer steady. "It was the—signature that did it. Sorry. I'll be all right in a moment."

They sat in Lucille's study while Lucille read the letter aloud. There was no salutation and no date, but the word-processor printing was impeccable. "'Since by law my safe-deposit box will only be opened in the presence of a tax man,'" the letter began, "'I am confident that this will reach you. Maybe I'm being too melodramatic, but I don't think so. For reasons as

83

yet unclear, I believe my life is threatened. I imagine this will come as no surprise to a number of people, and maybe not even to you. I remember your pointing out, individually and jointly, a number of times, that the ability to get along with people was not transmitted in the genes, but was something that had to be learned. Obviously I have never learned it.'"

Lucille stopped reading here and swallowed hard as she stared for a long silent moment out her window at the stunning view of the great mountains. But when at last she spoke, her voice was under control. "Self-assessment," she said. "I am not sure I would have expected that."

Waldo said, "Does he develop his suspicions?"

The letter did not. "'With insufficient data,'" Lucille read on, "'speculation on either specific motives or the specific person or persons involved is pointless. Nor have I sufficient grounds even to make contact with the police. They have no reason to think very highly of me and I can imagine their reactions, probably of amusement, something on the order of, "It couldn't happen to a nicer guy."'"

"So alone!" Lucille said.

"We tried."

"Not hard enough. No, strike that. We tried, and we failed." Epitaph. She took up the letter sheets and began to read again.

"'If you have not already learned, you will soon, that there is to be established in my name a trust to oversee the disposition of the cash and continuing royalties from the sale of CH Company. I have named you both as trustees, and I hope you will accept the responsibility. You, far better than I, will know how best to distribute the trust's assets, and so in the trust agreement drawn with the bank, I have not imposed restrictions that might in any way hamper your judgments. Joe Whitney, my lawyer, also a trustee, will be able to advise you on guidelines that will manage to keep the trust in a nonprofit, tax-exempt status.

" 'You will also learn that you are the named beneficiaries of my life insurance policy. This is in no sense an act of contrition; I have gone my way, by my lights, and I apologize to no one. But I admire you both, and I know of no two persons who better deserve some kind of unasked-for reward for being what they are. Accept the money, and enjoy it.' "

Lucille's voice stopped abruptly, and she sat motionless and silent again for long moments, staring not at the window and the view, but, unseeing, out into the room. She said at last in a voice that again was not quite steady, "He added a word, printed in his own hand." She looked then at Waldo. "The word is in capital letters, and underlined, with an exclamation point. *PLEASE!*"

Waldo took off his glasses, looked at them, and put them back on again. He said nothing.

"I'm not sure I can handle this," Lucille Harrington said slowly. "I—" She stopped again and was silent, looking still at her husband. For a long time neither spoke.

It was Waldo who said at last, "I believe we have no choice."

Lucille took a long, deep breath. She nodded slowly. "You are right. We *can* handle it, and we will."

"Read on," Waldo said.

Lucille picked up the letter again. " 'Joe Whitney,' " she read, " 'has advised me in all these matters, and I believe that his advice has been sound. At times I have

85

been tempted to believe that I was far more worldly than I am, and Joe has set me straight. Other times, I have not known how to proceed in the face of legal complications, and again Joe has come to the rescue. I commend him to you if these new responsibilities I have laid upon you take you at times out of your areas of competence.

" 'Lastly, I ask a personal favor which I hope you will not find too onerous. There is a girl named Penelope Lincoln, an artist, although not a very good one. Sid Thomas taught me better than he knew how to recognize artistic dross. But I have enjoyed the company of Penny the person, and I hope and trust that our association has not placed her in any jeopardy. If it turns out that it has, I ask that you do what you can to help her.

" 'Thank you for your patience.' "

Lucille put the letter face down on her desk. "He signs it formally, Charles Harrington."

Waldo got up from his chair. His voice was quiet and unemotional. "I think a martini and some music on the *portal* while we watch the sunset and assess the situation. Agreed?"

Lucille rose too. Her face was again composed. "You mix the martinis. I will choose the music. I think Tchaikovsky. *Pathétique.*"

Ross Cathcart flew to Mexico City the day after he was released from the hospital. Johnny Ortiz heard about it from Tony Lopez who, through a vast network of friends and relatives, usually managed to know almost everything that happened in Santo Cristo as soon as it took place.

"Damn," Johnny said. "Mexico City's a big place."

"I have heard," Tony said. Except for army service in Texas, he had never been more than 200 miles from Santo Cristo.

Johnny was already reaching for the phone and dialing swiftly. When Cassie answered, "Cathcart," Johnny said. "You met him once in Mexico City, *chica,* no? And you mentioned a hotel. At which one does he stay?" He wrote quickly on a pad of paper, tore off the top sheet, and tucked it in his pocket. *"Bueno.* Thanks. I won't be home tonight." He pushed back his chair and stood up.

Just like that, Tony thought, and not for the first time was caught off-balance. Because this was the way *Anglos* behaved, making instant decisions and acting on the moment. He, himself, preferred to ponder a choice, savor it, and when in due course the decision was made, move ahead without unseemly haste. In his experience, Indians too, Navajo, Apache, Zuñi, Hopi, or Pueblo, tended to behave in similar dignified if not stately fashion. It took time to get oneself into the proper frame of mind; that was the long and the short of it. But this Juan Felipe Ortiz, Anglo, Spanish, and Indian rarely followed any rules, which was disconcerting. He—

"See you," Johnny said, and was gone.

Cassie found the house empty-seeming that evening, and Chico too seemed to feel the lack. As he paced around the rooms he wore a disconsolate air, and in the end he came back to Cassie and stayed close beside her as she went about producing a lonely dinner.

Not all that long ago, of course, she had lived in this same house, alone and enjoying the privacy and sense of independence. And she was the same person now, was she not? Face it, she told herself, you're not. Strangely, she felt no pain in the admission.

Johnny, she thought, was no longer the same person, either, and she wondered if he realized it. Busy people rarely gave much thought to human relations; they seemed to take them as they came, without doubt or question, and that was that. It was only occasionally, as now, eating automatically and scarcely tasting her food, that a sudden need for assessment arose and odd thoughts began to crowd into her mind. It—

Chico sat up suddenly, ears pricked forward with intense interest. He made a sound, part whimpering whuffle, part subdued bark, and what that meant, Cassie could only guess.

And then the door opened and Johnny walked in, his face a frozen mask of anger. He closed the door very gently, and when he spoke, his voice was under careful control. "Hello, *chica*. As you see, I'm back." He shook his head then, the subdued anger plain. "No. That's wrong. I never went anywhere."

Cassie got up from the table, her meal forgotten. Never, she thought, had she seen him like this, right on the brink of explosion. "I'll light the fire," she said, and was astonished that her voice sounded as calm as it did. "Then we can sit, and you can tell me about it, yes?" The question held a plea.

"Chica—" The word came out with effort. Slowly, very slowly, some of the tension went out of his shoulders, and the harsh lines of his face began to relax. "Yes," he said. "That is what I need."

They sat companionably close, but not touching, on the sofa facing the fire. Chico rested his chin on

Johnny's foot and watched his people quietly, rolling his eyes from one to the other as they spoke.

"Obviously they were primed," Johnny said. "Feds. Maybe Customs—" He shook his head. "They didn't volunteer much information, but they were Treasury. And they had their orders." For a moment the harsh lines were very plain again. "I was out of my territory, of course, just another Joe Citizen. They made that plain."

"But—what?" Cassie said. "What on earth—?"

"Simple. Cathcart had gone to Mexico City. They were seeing to it that I didn't go too."

"Mark Hawley?"

"Who else? He's a tough old bird." There was even a hint of admiration in the words. "He knows his way around. And he's thorough. He warned me. Now he showed me some muscle." He was silent for a few moments, staring at the fire. "The message is plain: Lay off Cathcart."

"Do you know why?"

"No. All I have are guesses, and not very good ones at that."

"But if he is involved—"

"In Charley Harrington's murder? Yes. Possible." He was silent again, watching the flames as if in them he could see a reflection of his own thoughts and his mood. At last he could relax and even smile as he turned to look at Cassie. "I'm walking around in the dark, *chica.* Both too much and too little to make any sense out of any of it yet."

"But you will." A confident statement of immutable fact.

* * *

Sam herself was behind the bar, and she answered the phone, listened quietly without expression, and then, looking across the crowded barroom, caught Penny Lincoln's eye and held up the phone. Penny got up slowly and came to answer it.

It was a short, largely one-sided conversation, ending with, "I guess so. Okay. Sure." Penny hung up, went back across the room to pick up her jacket, and walked out into the night. Sam watched her go.

Penny drove without haste along the familiar route. On this night she felt no particular sense of anticipation, but neither was there any feeling of reluctance. These last few days she had been living in a state of suspended animation, time standing still, and the world a strange, alien place.

If she had been asked, she would have denied that she missed Charley Harrington. Maybe that red Ferrari of his, and the good places he took her, and perhaps some of the things they did together in the privacy of her tiny studio, but not the man himself; he, as a person, had not been that important. As far as that went, nobody was really that important. It was just that, well, she didn't like to be alone; that was the heart of the matter.

She parked, as always, on the street, not in the long, curving drive, and walked up to the large house. Grace Cathcart herself answered the bell and produced one of her rare smiles as she held the door wide. "A long time," Grace Cathcart said, as she closed the door solidly after the girl.

Grace wore a pale blue silk robe and matching mules that went well with her blond hair and fair skin. Wordlessly she led the way past the living room and

Ross Cathcart's study, down the hallway, and into her bedroom, where she closed the door after them.

It was a large bedroom with a king-size bed, now neatly turned down. Grace took off her robe and laid it on the back of a chair. Her slim, sleek, smoothly contoured body was naked, and she smiled as she turned to face Penny. "I thought a nice, hot bath," she said, "and then we can enjoy ourselves on the bed." Again that rare smile. "Yes?"

"Sure. Okay." Penny was already undressing, tossing the jacket on a chair, peeling off the tank top to expose her large, full, firm breasts. Automatically she posed for a moment to allow Grace to study her in smiling admiration before kicking off her shoes and bending over to slip out of her jeans and briefs. As she straightened, naked, she felt at last the end of loneliness, and in her loins and breasts the tingling beginning of anticipatory pleasure.

"I've missed you," Grace said as she held out her hand. Her voice was soft, fond. "Come along. The bath is all ready."

Cassie lay awake for a long time that night, carefully controlling her breathing to make it sound as if she slept, while she stared up at the darkness and her thoughts.

She had never interfered in any of Johnny's work, and she was sure he would resent it if she did. His male pride was deep and solid, and when she thought about it, she was not at all sure that she wished it were otherwise. As an anthropologist, her views of the differences between men and women were not those of the more aggressive women liberationists, and as

Cassie Enright the person, she liked things pretty much the way they were.

On the other hand, it was clear that Johnny was frustrated by whatever had happened at the airport when he had been prevented from boarding a plane bound for Mexico—it must have been, Cassie thought, smiling now, a fairly stormy scene—and she disliked thinking about the possible directions his reaction might take. When aroused, she knew, he was prone to violent action, and, as he had said himself, Mark Hawley was a tough old bird with considerable power he was not afraid to use.

I am damned if I do, Cassie thought, and I will be tormented if I don't. That summed it up neatly, and she felt better as she closed her eyes at last and went almost immediately off to sleep.

8

Congressman Mark Hawley leaned back in his chair and nodded; not unfriendly, merely wary. "I kind of expected you, son," he said, and took his time studying Johnny's face. "I wasn't exactly sure what your mood would be, but you don't look too hostile. Have a chair. I expect you want to talk?"

Johnny sat down. He admired the old man. Hawley was never one to evade an issue. He could be devious and, like the first-rate poker player he was, could run a bluff without shame or hesitation. On the other hand, his word once given was his bond, and fear of consequences was not in his nature.

"You're after Cathcart," Johnny said. "You as much as told me that up at Flora's. Using the Feds to tie me down made it just about certain." He studied the old man's face. It showed nothing. "Am I right so far?"

"You're doing the talking, son. I'm listening."

"I'm only interested in who killed Charley Harrington, and why. Cathcart turns up too often to suit me."

The congressman was silent for a time, his face as blank as a mirror. "I'll tell you one thing, son," he said at last. "Cathcart couldn't have killed young Harrington. He wasn't anywhere in the vicinity."

"Or had him killed," Johnny said.

The congressman's face did show interest then, and he was silent again, thinking hard. "To be honest, that hadn't occurred to me," he said. "Tell me why."

"I don't know. There was the tapped phone line—"

"Dwell on that, son," the congressman said. His interest had quickened now, and he listened attentively.

"That's news to me," he said when Johnny was done. "Charley never mentioned that."

"I haven't gone to the phone company yet," Johnny said. "But I will. This time we'll find out for sure—" He stopped and shook his head. "Maybe we won't at that. Harrington—"

"You have a point," the congressman said. "Charley knew his way around electronically, the way they call it today, like maybe only a handful of folks in this whole area including those up at the Scientific Lab. If he wanted to tap a phone and didn't want it found out—" He spread his hands. "The Langley people tell me there are ways and ways and more ways that are right near impossible to find."

"So maybe we're back to Cathcart."

The congressman heaved himself out of his chair and walked across the office to a cupboard. From it he took a bottle and two glasses and carried them back to his desk. He poured each glass with care and pushed one across to Johnny. "Maybe," he said at last, "and maybe not. You're fishing, son, and maybe you've found the right fishing hole and maybe you haven't, but until we know—" He picked up his glass. *"Salud,"* he said. "I like the way you follow a trail. But you're going to have to come up with more than you have now before I'll go the whole way with you." He watched Johnny's face. "You're not against drinking with me?"

"No," Johnny said. He picked up his glass. "There's enough Anglo in me for that."

He walked back to police headquarters from the federal building in a thoughtful mood. Tony Lopez was waiting for him, and Tony's expression was uncharacteristically somber. "There was a phone call," Tony said. "For you." He hesitated, and Johnny waited in silence, his eyes fixed on Tony's face.

Tony took a deep breath. "Cassie Enright," he said.

"What about her?"

"She was calling from the airport. She didn't have much time. Her flight—"

"Where was she going?" But already, Johnny thought, he knew the answer, and anger like a warm flood filled his mind. "Mexico City," he said and watched Tony's reluctant nod.

Johnny walked into his office and reached for the telephone as he sat down. He punched the number with swift savagery. The congressman himself answered. "You had the Feds stop me," Johnny said. "Did you tell them to stop Cassie too?"

There was a pause. Johnny could almost see the old man thinking over the situation. "No, son, I didn't. Should I have?"

"She's gone. What is she walking into?"

"Now, son—"

"I asked a question, goddamnit. Is she in danger if she starts asking questions down there? She knows Cathcart. She knows where he stays. She—"

"Simmer down. I don't know the answers. But I'll see what I can do."

"You'd better. Or I—"

"You just sit tight, son." The congressman's voice had taken on a sudden edge. "You're the hell of a good man. I know that. But you're not going down to Mexico, and that's final. If I have to, I'll have you locked up so you can't go anywhere. *Entendido?*"

Johnny hung up and sat quiet, staring at the wall and forcing the anger he felt back into its lair. He was not aware that Tony stood in the doorway, watching. He was not aware of anything but his own thoughts and worries. If anything happened to Cassie, *anything* —he made himself stop that thought because it was futile and distracting. He forced himself to concentrate not on what might be, but on what was.

Cathcart was gone. But Cathcart had a wife, and sometimes wives would talk when husbands would not. Had Cathcart left his wife behind when he flew off to Mexico City? He was unaware that he spoke the question aloud.

"Yes," Tony Lopez said. "She doesn't usually go with him on business trips. My *prima*—" He stopped. Johnny's face said plainly that he did not care to hear what Tony's cousin had to say. "The address," Tony said, "is Old Agua Fría Road. Big house. You can't miss it."

Johnny was already at the door. He stopped and turned back into the office. "Glenn Ronson," he said. There were, after all, two murders, not just one. And the fact that a shotgun had been used both times tied them together. And Cathcart again came into both. "Any known enemies? Money problems? Debts?" Another thought suddenly appearing, unbidden. "Any known tie to Charley Harrington?"

"Bueno," Tony said. His tone was resigned. "I will sift the rumors."

"I'll be at the Cathcart house."

"You know, *amigo,*" Tony said, "somehow I guessed that already."

Grace Cathcart, wearing the blue silk robe and high-heeled mules, answered Johnny's knock. Johnny had his badge in his hand. He held it up, and she merely glanced at it. "My husband is not at home," she said. Her calm eyes studied him appraisingly. "Lieutenant Ortiz, no? I . . . have heard of you."

"I know where your husband is. I want to talk to you."

"This is not a convenient time, Lieutenant. Perhaps—"

"Now."

Grace Cathcart's rare smile appeared briefly. "The domineering male, Lieutenant?" She stepped back and held the door wide. "I am helpless. Do come in."

It was, Johnny thought, an opulent house, even ostentatious. He knew little about such things, but he would have been willing to bet that the Oriental rug in the living room, twelve feet by fifteen at a guess, would command at least a five-figure price; a huge Fritz Scholder painting dominated one wall; and a free-standing bronze sculpture of what he took to be something on the order of a phoenix stood at one side of the large fireplace, reminding him that among other

97

things, Cathcart owned an art gallery here in town. Every piece of furniture in the large room showed both money and taste.

Grace Cathcart arranged herself on a settee. Johnny took an overstuffed chair from which he could see the window and a glimpse of the road. Movement outside caught his eye, and he glanced at it long enough to recognize Penny Lincoln hurrying toward the nondescript car he had seen parked a little distance away. He remembered what Sam had said about the girl. Well, well, he thought.

"Well, Lieutenant?" Grace Cathcart said. "You wanted to talk to me?" If she had seen him looking outside, she gave no indication.

"Your house was broken into," Johnny said. "Ransacked, was the report."

"It was a mess." For the first time Grace Cathcart showed emotion—anger. "I am proud of my house, Lieutenant, and I resented the condition we found it in."

"But nothing was taken." Johnny looked around the room. Every tabletop had its small treasure: a jeweled silver box here, a small jade sculpture there, a stunning ivory figurine in yet another individual display; an intricately carved translucent stone chess set occupied its own inlaid chessboard tabletop. "With all these things, nothing taken." He watched the woman's face and waited.

"Nothing." Grace Cathcart was obviously still angry, but the anger was held under tight control. "I am attached to my possessions, Lieutenant, and I know them intimately. I would have known instantly if anything were missing."

"Then why do you suppose the break-in?"

"I have absolutely no idea. Nor has my husband."

"So he said when I talked to him in the hospital."

The calm eyes studied Johnny's face carefully. "But you didn't believe him, is that it, Lieutenant? May I ask why?" She shook her head quickly, dismissing her own question. "No doubt you had your reasons. Do you mind my saying, Lieutenant, that you have the face of a sculpture? Aztec, I should think, or perhaps even Mayan?"

"Apache." A formidable woman, Johnny was thinking, used to being in control in most situations. Thinking of Penny Lincoln, he decided that the dominant personality figured. "Your husband," he said, "also believed that his phone was tapped, didn't he?"

Grace Cathcart seemed suddenly off-balance. "Did he tell you that?"

"Apparently it upset him," Johnny said. "Maybe even more than would have seemed necessary. Would you know why?"

She took her time, gathering herself, Johnny thought, but her eyes did not fall away from his, and he could admire her for that. A strong woman, he thought again, used to being in control not only of situations, but also of herself. "In a word," she said, "no, I do not know."

"Your husband's business—"

"He is a commodities trader, Lieutenant. The fact is widely known."

"He discusses business with you?"

The rare smile appeared again. It was, Johnny decided, a smile of triumph. "Never," she said.

99

"I find that hard to believe. Between husband and wife—"

"Suit yourself, Lieutenant." The smile held. "But the answer is still the same. We do not discuss my husband's business. We talk about art, music, books, the theater—we are just back, as you may know, from a spate of theater-going in London. Do you wish to know what plays and shows we saw? The Shaw revival, of course, and—" She stopped. "But I'm afraid I bore you, Lieutenant. I apologize."

"Yes," Johnny said, and with difficulty refrained from the uneducated singsong Spanish accent he could affect when he said, "Culture is not my specialty." He watched her smile fade a little. "Your husband is a nervous man, isn't he? Easily upset? He—"

"My husband is not a nervous man, Lieutenant." The smile was entirely gone now. "Nor is he easily upset. The business of trading commodities puts great strain on a person, and my husband withstands that strain admirably. He—"

"And yet he came apart when he found the house ransacked. Why would that be, Mrs. Cathcart? Particularly since it was determined that nothing was taken?"

"What my husband experienced—"

"Was severe atrial fibrillations, almost certainly stress-related. The question is, what caused the sudden stress?"

There was anger again now, held under tight control. "You are a doctor, Lieutenant?"

"No, Mrs. Cathcart. But I talk to doctors. Asking questions is my business. Asking, and listening to the answers." He was getting to her, he thought, and exactly what that might accomplish, he had no idea, but it did give him an advantage. "So a sudden collapse does raise questions. You can see that, I'm sure."

Grace Cathcart breathed deeply twice, but again her eyes did not leave Johnny's. "Lieutenant," she said in her normal calm voice, patiently explaining the obvious, "my husband and I had just returned from a long, and somewhat arduous trip. We had been in Scotland—"

"Fishing, yes. And theater-going in London, as you said. And there was no doubt jet lag involved, the seven hour time-change. Yes. And then to find your house-sitter gone, and the house torn apart—" Johnny stopped and smiled. "Naturally upsetting."

"You put it well, Lieutenant." The anger was barely controlled. "Do you have any other unnecessary questions?"

"Not right now," Johnny said. He stood up and looked around. "A lovely home. A showplace. You must be very proud of it."

"I will show you to the door," Grace Cathcart said.

Johnny was in no hurry walking out to his car. Cassie was again in his mind, and it was difficult to think of anything else. He could call her in Mexico City at the hotel whose name she had given him. But what would that accomplish even if he were lucky enough to make immediate contact? If Cassie had made up her mind to go to Mexico in his place, as obviously she had, then, being the person she was, she would not back off just because of a phone call. Even from him. Johnny had seen her before with her mind made up.

Cathcart, Johnny thought, was going to have a lot of answering to do if anything were to happen to Cassie —Congressman Hawley or no Congressman Hawley. And that futile thought, he told himself, was all he could do at the moment in that direction.

He got into his four-wheel-drive pickup, started the engine, and then just sat for a few moments deciding which direction he wanted to go now. The decision was made for him.

The car radio came on with its hollow carrier-wave sound, and Tony Lopez's voice said, "Calling Lieutenant Ortiz. Lieutenant Ortiz, come in."

Johnny took up the microphone and pressed the button. "Ortiz here."

"You've got a visitor," Tony's voice said. "Joe Whitney, the lawyer. He says it's important."

"Ten-four. On my way."

Whitney was waiting in Johnny's office. He was as affable as he had been at their first meeting, but there was an undertone of gravity in his manner that had not been there before. He seemed also, Johnny thought, almost hesitant.

"I have given this matter a great deal of thought, Lieutenant," he said, "and I finally decided that I was almost obligated to come to you as a citizen, and as a lawyer, an officer of the court."

Johnny waited in silence.

"There is a man," Whitney said, "with whom Charley Harrington had . . . dealings. I use the word advisedly. In matters not connected with his actual technical work, which I did not even pretend to understand, Charley relied rather heavily on me. He was, as you must realize, a highly intelligent person, Lieutenant, but he realized his limitations, which is unusual in anyone, most particularly in someone of Charley's acumen."

"Dealings," Johnny said without inflection. "What kind of dealings?"

"Highly—ah—unusual," Whitney said. "I will admit that I did not inquire into them too deeply. Between us, frankly, I didn't want to know if Charley was doing something that was improper or illegal. You can appreciate that."

Nothing changed in Johnny's face. "Go on," he said.

"From this man," Whitney said, speaking more slowly now, and choosing his words with care, "Charley at times obtained money. I am not exactly sure how, or why, but the money was forthcoming and Charley used it."

"For what?"

"For his CH Company. Especially in the early days, before I was even associated in a professional way with Charley, there were times when he needed money badly. Most new, small companies do."

"He had ways of raising it," Johnny said.

Whitney opened his mouth and shut it again carefully. "I am not sure I understand you, Lieutenant."

"I think you do. Bert Clancy—"

Whitney let his breath out, and smiled. "I see," he said. "That money, Lieutenant, was always paid back, punctiliously, with interest."

"And charges were never brought."

"A holding company decision. They wanted no publicity."

"So," Johnny said, "Charley had this big financial cow he could milk whenever he wanted. Why this—other man?"

"I am not clear on that, Lieutenant. Charley was always . . . evasive on that subject, and, as I said before, I didn't want to pry too deeply."

Bert Clancy had said as much, Johnny thought; Clancy had said that you could fool even good accountants for a time, but that sooner or later they would catch up with you, and there were definitely funds Charley had for his company that had not come from Bert Clancy's bank. So it figured. "Did Charley Harrington pay back these funds?" he said.

"I very much doubt it, Lieutenant. I can't say for sure. When it came to figures, Charley could baffle anyone. But this money appeared, and was used, and as far as I know no records of it were kept."

"Hot money? Laundered money? Is that what you're saying?"

Whitney was uncomfortable. "Lieutenant, I was never a part of these—ah—transactions. I knew that they existed, that's all. I wanted no part of them."

Johnny thought about it. "All right," he said, "understood. Charley raised money from time to time. You don't know how, or why. You doubt if it was ever paid back. You think maybe somebody got tired of being taken, and reacted? With a shotgun?"

Whitney drew a deep breath. "The possibility had occurred to me, Lieutenant. I . . . hesitate to make charges I cannot substantiate. But—"

"I take it," Johnny said, "that we're talking about substantial sums of money? How much, at a guess? Ten thousand dollars? Fifty thousand?" It was a question he could put to Bert Clancy too, he thought.

"I would think at least the latter amount, Lieutenant, but, as I said, I—"

"Was careful not to know too much." Johnny

104

nodded. Concepts of conscience or morality had different meanings to different folks, he thought, which was handy. "Okay. The man's name, Counselor?"

"You understand, Lieutenant, that I am not making any charges? As I said, I have given this matter considerable thought, and I decided that it was my— duty to come to you. But I do not want to open myself to charges of slander."

"Of course not."

"The man is very prominent," Whitney said. "He is a businessman, a very successful businessman. He also owns—"

"An art gallery?" Johnny said. It almost had to be. It all fitted too neatly to be otherwise. He watched Whitney's face begin to come apart like a photograph overenlarged, and he waited in silence.

"I take it," Whitney said at last, "that you know the man of whom I speak?"

"I think Ross Cathcart would be a pretty good guess, wouldn't it?"

Whitney got out a white handkerchief. He dabbed at his forehead, clearly uncomfortable now.

"Well?" Johnny said. "Is it Cathcart?"

Whitney nodded slowly. "Yes, Lieutenant." His tone was reluctant. "I am afraid it is."

Tony Lopez came in after Whitney had gone. "The broker I talked to says Cathcart is a high roller, almost entirely in commodities—pork bellies, whatever they are—but occasionally into stocks—equities, he calls them—and runs his own show. They know him here only by reputation."

"No rumors of fast dealing?" Johnny said.

Tony flashed white teeth in a wide grin. "I asked him that. He said with the stories coming out of Wall Street these days, he wouldn't swear his own mother's hands were clean. Cathcart means big bucks, and what that means—" Tony shrugged hugely and spread his hands.

Johnny reached for the telephone and called Bert Clancy at the bank. "You mentioned cash not accounted for that Charley Harrington used in his company, no?"

Bert Clancy took his time answering. At last, "Yes. That's right."

"Big money?"

"Big enough. Discrepancies like that are hard to pin down, but, yes, considerable sums were unaccounted for."

"One more question," Johnny said. "Have Waldo and Lucille Harrington come to you?"

Again Clancy's voice was cautious. "They have."

"And?"

"I gave them what I properly could."

"Give them whatever you have," Johnny said. "They're a lot better at figures than I'll ever be, and their conclusions could be helpful. If you need a court order—" He left the sentence unfinished.

Again there was that hesitation. "Oh, hell," Bert Clancy said, "I want to get to the bottom of this just as much as you do, so I'll stretch a few points."

Johnny hung up and leaned back in his chair to look up at Tony Lopez. "You're always hearing rumors," he said. "What do you hear about Grace Cathcart?"

"Like what?"

"I'm not exactly sure." He told Tony about seeing Penny Lincoln hurrying down to her car, and what Sam had said about the girl. "Penny Lincoln and Charley Harrington," he went on, "Penny Lincoln and Grace Cathcart; Grace Cathcart and Cathcart— mean anything to you?" He would much rather have put the question to Cassie, he thought, but Cassie was in Mexico City, and again the anger was stirring. He looked at Tony and waited.

Tony shook his head slowly. "Only," he said, "that there are a lot of things about women I don't understand."

"Claro." Johnny thought about it briefly, but the flicker of thought that had been in his mind had disappeared without a trace, and trying to force it back into the open would merely be an exercise in futility, so he let it go. "Glenn Ronson—anything?"

Tony consulted his notebook. "Lived alone. Ate organic foods, whatever they are. No known enemies. No known close friends, as far as that goes. Liked animals, dogs, cats, just about anything. Had a pet skunk once, until the neighbors raised hell." He closed the notebook with a snap. "You think he was killed for his keys, the key to the Cathcart house?"

"Quién sabe? But if he was, then Cathcart hardly figures, and every time I turn around Cathcart is there." He made a short, sharp gesture dismissing Cathcart. "Double-ought buckshot," he said. "Anything?"

Tony shook his head. "Nobody in town carries it. No call for it." Tony was thoughtful. "Only man I ever knew used double-ought buckshot was a fellow ran sheep over near Pecos. Whenever he got a shot at a coyote, he didn't want to miss."

The phone rang on Johnny's desk. He picked it up and spoke his name. It was Cassie, and her voice was faint, a bad connection. *"Chica—"* Johnny began in a louder-than-usual tone, and then stopped. She would tell him what she wanted to tell. "I'm listening," he said, and made himself sit quiet, staring at the wall.

"I'm in Mexico City. You know that. I've seen Cathcart. I'm . . . having dinner with him tonight. He still thinks his charm will win out. It won't."

Johnny took a deep breath and let it out slowly. He said nothing.

"Did you hear me?" Cassie said.

"I heard. Damn it, *chica,* I don't want you there. I don't know what's going on, but if it's important enough for Hawley to put pressure on the Feds—"

"But I am here," Cassie said. "So the rest doesn't count, does it?" She could be infuriating in her irrefutable logic. "He likes to talk. I like to listen. I'll be in touch. Don't forget to feed Chico. *Hasta luego.*"

"Oh, hell," Johnny said.

"I've heard better goodbyes."

"Take care of yourself," Johnny said, "hear?"

"That's better. Promise." The line went dead.

Johnny hung up, pushed back his chair, and stood up. All at once inactivity was unbearable. "I'm going for a walk." He looked hard at Tony and waited for comment.

Expressionless, "I'll mind the store," Tony said.

Johnny walked outside into the brisk October air and breathed deeply as a man might when first freed from confinement. He had no direction in mind as he began to walk, but when he found himself on the winding road that led past Sid Thomas's studio, it was evident that, as almost always, his subconscious mind was giving directions. It had always amused him that some called it inspiration.

Sid was in and glowering at his easel on which stood the almost finished painting of that corner of the Palace of the Governors Johnny had seen that first day.

"Set, son," Sid said, "and tell me what's on your mind." He seated himself and began to suck placidly on his oxygen.

"When Charley was just a kid," Johnny said, "apparently he tapped a telephone line. Would you have any idea why?"

Sid rumpled his fringe of white hair while he thought about it. "Nope," he said at last. "Except that he was always trying new things, electrical things, just to see how they worked. He sat and watched me one day, asking questions like he always did. I wasn't paying much attention to what he was doing, painting like I was and trying to answer his questions, and first thing I knew he had my phone in pieces all laid out neat on that table next to you, funny-looking things I never knew were inside a phone, never thought about before." He had another long pull on the oxygen.

"Did he put it back together again?" Johnny said.

"Oh, sure. Worked even better than before. He'd got rid of a kind of hum that had been there for a long time."

Interesting, Johnny thought, but hardly important. "Did he ever mention a fellow named Cathcart, Ross Cathcart?"

Sid's expression changed. "Fellow owns the gallery? That one?"

Johnny nodded and held his breath. Had he hit pay dirt?

"Nope," Sid said. His expression showed unmistakable anger, which was strange, because Johnny had never seen Sid angry before. His even temper was legendary. "Charley didn't even know him," Sid added, biting off the words as if they tasted bad.

"How could you be sure of that?" Johnny said. "Charley seemed to get around, even as a kid."

"Because I mentioned Cathcart one day, and Charley didn't pay any attention like he'd never even heard of him."

There was something here, and Johnny had no idea what it was, but it was his experience that when a trail took a strange turn it sometimes paid to follow it to see where it led. "But you knew Cathcart, Sid?"

More oxygen, and slow relaxation. "I knew him," Sid said. "Had my paintings in his gallery once. Had me an exhibition. Quite a few sales. Just that once."

"Why? If it was successful, why only once?"

Sid had a final pull on the oxygen. "I'm not much at figures," he said. "But it seems like he skinned me good, charged more than he told me for each painting, and pocketed the difference." He heaved himself out of his chair. "Happens," he said. "Everybody knows artists aren't maybe too smart when it comes to business. Most artists, that is. Back to work, son. But stick around if you like. Won't bother me a bit."

Johnny too had risen. Something was crawling around in his mind. "I have to go. Just one more question. When that happened, the Cathcart thing, did you know Charley Harrington?"

Sid thought about it. "I disremember. Long time ago. He—" He stopped and his face cleared. "Nope. I do remember. It was just about then that Charley began to hang around here, started asking his questions. Maybe that's how it all began. He kind of took my mind off being sore about Cathcart and the money." He smiled sadly. "Charley was like maybe you'd say therapeutic."

"Thanks, Sid," Johnny said, and got a wave of a brush in response.

He was thinking hard as he walked back down the winding dirt road, and again his subconscious was apparently directing his footsteps, because he found himself standing in front of Sam's bar. He hesitated only a moment before he went in.

Sam was at a table by herself, a cup of coffee in front of her. "Hi, stranger. Pull up a chair. How's hunting?"

Johnny sat down. Sam was unmistakably woman—the Valkyrie came to mind—but there was a masculine directness to her that took away the awareness of sex differences. Johnny looked around the bar. Penny Lincoln was nowhere in sight.

Sam smiled. "Looking for Penny? She comes in nights. Most nights."

"I saw her a while back." Johnny kept his voice uninflected.

"That so?" Sam studied his face. "What're you saying, *amigo?*"

"She was leaving the Cathcart house."

Sam sipped her coffee. Her eyes did not leave Johnny's face. "You asking a question?"

"Ross Cathcart's in Mexico."

"So I heard." Sam set her coffee cup down very gently. "But the wife isn't. Good-looking woman. I'll give her that. Keeps herself up well. Dresses well. Drives a big car. Has money to spend." Sam picked up a pack of cigarettes from the tabletop, shook one out with expert ease, and took her time tapping and lighting it. She blew smoke off to the side and looked again at Johnny. "I don't mess much in other folks' business, *amigo,* but I do notice things. Does that answer your question?"

"Pretty much."

"I told you what Penny is, a mixed-up kid, trying to be an artist which she won't ever be, broke or near enough most of the time. She only has one thing to sell, and when you're in that fix, your choices are pretty much limited. Marriage is the way out for some, maybe most. I wouldn't know." Sam smiled without amusement. "I told you. I figured out my way a long time ago, just like you figured out yours. Penny hasn't got there yet and maybe never will."

Johnny surprised himself. "That sounds like an epitaph." He pushed back his chair and stood up.

Sam was looking up at him. "Maybe it is, at that. Wouldn't surprise me. See you, *amigo.*"

"Thanks, Sam." He walked again out into the brisk October day.

His subconscious took him this time to the plaza, where he sat down on a bench. Automatically he glanced up at the great mountains with the masses of golden aspen among the forest of evergreens on their slopes. The cathedral bell tolled the hour and the sonorous notes hung in the air like echoes. A raven flew past, squawking his harsh protest. A house sparrow, clean and sharply clothed in his brown and white with black bib, hopped close, cocked an eye at Johnny, decided he was not a good bet for crumbs, and flew away. Johnny was oblivious.

A Cathcart here, a Cathcart there, everywhere a Cathcart—as in the song. But the pieces of the puzzle still did not fit.

Cassie was in Mexico and in a few hours would be dining with Cathcart and listening to him. Was there —danger there? Mark Hawley had said he would see what he could do, and Hawley was to be believed. Unless— No, that thought passed quickly, rejected out of hand. There could not be any connection between Cathcart and Hawley other than the one that was obvious, that Hawley's interest was official, probably arising out of one of the innumerable committees he sat on in Congress; oversight committees, some of them, looking over the shoulders of the various law-enforcement agencies of the government, seeing files and reports on people like Cathcart—doing what?

Penny Lincoln and Grace Cathcart, lovers without a doubt. Sam had confirmed that, almost in so many words. So? Johnny had no prurient interest in the fact, only in its implications. And again he wished Cassie were here to talk to, because in a vague sort of way he was sure that only another woman would be able to understand, even if she were not inclined that way herself, something of the rapport that might be between two lovers.

Usually, Johnny knew, one of the pair was dominant. That would be Grace Cathcart. Penny would prefer to be told, directed. But how far would that relationship extend? Would there be, for example, confidences between them during periods of relaxed respite? Maybe comments on men in general whom they locked out of their own intimate world? And if so, where did that lead?

Basta! he told himself. Enough! You are charging off into uncharted territory where you don't know your head from a hot rock. Still, the feeling remained strong that there was food for thought in that area, although he could not have said why. Damn, he wished Cassie were here—for more reasons than one!

Sid Thomas, now; why did he keep thinking peripherally about Sid? He was the one person in all of Santo Cristo, maybe the one person anywhere, who really had *known* Charley Harrington as a . . . friend, no? Yes! The concept of the ailing old man and the apparently difficult, precocious boy striking up any kind of relationship seemed almost too much, but Johnny believed strongly that they had been friends.

Well, where else might that spoor lead? How about

Will Carston? He and Sid were cronies and had been for these forty years. Might Sid have spoken about Charley to Will? Time and again in idle conversation, Johnny had noted often, seemingly unimportant things were sometimes said that turned out to be most germane when looked at out of context.

Bueno! Will Carston it would be.

Will Carston lived in an old, sprawling, meticulously restored and maintained adobe house surrounded by eight acres of valuable Santo Cristo real estate and enclosed by a seven-foot adobe wall in whose top the long-ago masons had imbedded broken glass to discourage intruders. The eight acres, consisting of lawns, flower beds, cactus displays, and a fine kitchen vegetable garden, required three fulltime gardeners.

Carston was originally from the East, but had lived in Santo Cristo for over forty of his seventy-odd years. He was a poet—Pulitzer laureate—and the author of a monumental study of the Spanish land grants in the Santo Cristo area. He was what once was called a gentleman of means.

A Spanish maid led Johnny through the house where Carston greeted him in his book-lined study.

"Iced tea?" Will Carston said, "or would you prefer something stronger?"

"I'm fine." Johnny sat down and wondered how to begin. He was always a trifle ill-at-ease in Will Carston's presence. The man's erudition, his courtly manners, and Eastern-accented speech were vaguely intimidating.

"You are wearing," Will Carston said, "what I believe Sid Thomas calls your 'scalping-knife' look. May I inquire the reason?"

"Charley Harrington. And Glenn Ronson."

Carston nodded gravely. "Murder most foul. I knew nothing of Ronson, but the Harrington boy for all his eccentricities was a person. What he might have been—" He stopped. "The saddest words in any tongue—'what might have been.'"

"You knew him through Sid?" Johnny said.

"Only casually. Sid was his only—confidante. An odd pair, you'll agree, Lieutenant. Figuratively speaking, the boy was still in knee pants when he and Sid struck up their friendly relationship. Strangely enough, it endured."

"Sid told me about it. The kid saw a connection between art and higher mathematics."

Carston nodded. "We discussed it once, among other things."

"Such as?"

Will Carston smiled. "Nothing very pertinent, I'm afraid. Like Robert Oppenheimer, young Harrington was fascinated by abstruse Oriental religions and philosophy. An astonishing boy."

All very interesting, Johnny thought, but it led nowhere. He was searching his mind for a direction to take in questioning. "What was that you asked?" he said. "It went right by me."

Carston repeated his question. "Did Sid tell you that in his recent, affluent years, young Harrington bought a number of Sid's paintings? At rather high rates which he established himself?"

"No." Johnny sat quiet, thinking about it. "I've been through his house," he said, "and there are no Sid Thomas paintings there."

"You will find them in the Fine Arts Museum. He donated them." Carston smiled. "Perhaps as tax-deductible gifts. I wouldn't know. But he had to be concerned with taxes. The gifts, by the way, were made under the condition of strict anonymity."

"Then how—?" Johnny stopped. "Of course, of course. You're on the museum board, aren't you?"

Carston smiled. "And I am betraying a confidence, but I doubt if it matters now."

Johnny was silent for a few moments, thinking hard. He said at last, "Is Sid well-off? It's hard to tell with an artist."

Carston sighed. "That is a painful subject. But the answer is no, Sid is not well-off. Sid, in fact, has been more or less bankrupt all his adult life. His paintings sell, but the money seems to—disappear. I gave up years ago asking where it goes. Sid simply does not know. Nor care." Carston studied Johnny's face quietly. "Do I see indications of cogitation, Lieutenant? Something I have said has struck a chord?"

"I don't know," Johnny said. "And that is simple truth." He stood up. "Thanks for your time."

"I haven't reached the point yet," Carston said in his courtly way, "where I feel I must ration it. You are quite welcome. And if I have contributed anything that may aid your investigation, I am delighted. Can you find your own way out?"

Johnny walked back through the big house with its tiled and polished floors, its heavy hand-crafted furniture, and its expanses of whitewashed wall space on which paintings, mostly by Southwestern artists and all of high quality, competed with an occasional, museum-mounted Southwestern Indian rug. Large windows cut into the massive walls gave glimpses of patios where fountains splashed, and tended borders of indigenous plants invited one to sink into the comfortable outdoor furniture and relax, totally removed from any sounds of traffic or neighborhood bustle.

The whole was an enclave of peace and tranquility isolated, as was Flora Hobb's house within its walls, from the rest of the ancient city. This, Johnny thought, was how the wealthy *Conquistadores* had lived in early Spanish colonial times, and how, he had heard, the wealthy in Spain still tended to live. Feudal splendor was the phrase that came to mind.

He was in a thoughtful mood as he walked back down into town. Santo Cristo was a city of opposites and of extremes. The thought arose unbidden. He was being ridiculously philosophical, he told himself immediately, but the thoughts persisted with a tenacity that would not be denied as if an inner voice were trying to tell him something.

Within the city there was great wealth, an astonishing amount of it, as he knew, and there was deep poverty as well. Three cultures—Spanish, Indian, and Anglo—and well over 400 years of recorded history, commencing with Coronado's expedition up from Mexico City in 1540, had shaped the area's character, as, Johnny decided, the city and its surroundings had at least helped to shape the characters of its inhabitants. It would be difficult to see how the overwhelming presence of the great mountains, limitless skies, and endless vistas could help but affect anyone who dwelt within their view and constant awareness of their enormous impact.

Perhaps it was because of the heightened awareness one felt in these surroundings that persons themselves seemed to stand out in bolder color and outline. Was there anything in that which bore on the puzzle he was trying to put together?

Certainly Charley Harrington, the centerpiece of the puzzle, had been remarkable—and remarkably multifaceted. There was the precocious and mischievous child with his list of juvenile offenses, his almost total lack of friends—Sid Thomas being the sole exception—his enormous talent and imagination, and yet the soft side of his personality too, that Will Carston had indicated when he spoke of the paintings the affluent Charley Harrington had bought, not for himself, but for donation to the Fine Arts Museum and, presumably, in order to provide income for Sid Thomas. What was one to make of that? Simple loyalty to his one friend?

And then there were the Harringtons themselves, Waldo and Lucille, certainly anything but run-of-the mill persons, world-class scientists, individuals of quiet force—Johnny had still not lost the impression Lucille Harrington's calm, perceptive, and controlled behavior had made upon him—and yet inept parents, by their own admissions totally unable to cope with Charley's behavior patterns.

Ross Cathcart too, and his wife, Grace, were persons who would stand out in almost any gathering if only for their polished exteriors, their tight emotional control, their *slickness,* both of them, as if they had been rubbed to a high gloss. Were they that way because of circumstances, or because of self-education, and if the latter, why had they felt it necessary to erect impenetrable barriers between themselves and the rest of the world? What might those barriers conceal? How far, for example, might Ross Cathcart go in possibly illegal directions without compunction? Would he suborn violence? Murder? And that, of course, brought Cassie again strongly to mind, and it was some time before Johnny could submerge his worries again.

How about Joseph Whitney, the lawyer? He had come forward, as he said, as a good citizen and as a lawyer, an officer of the court, to tell Johnny his suspicions if not in so many words, at least in sufficient scope and detail that his meaning was unmistakable—the pointing of an accusing finger straight at Cathcart. What was Johnny to make of that? Was there some hidden feeling of antagonism in Whitney against Cathcart? Stranger real motives had often turned up.

And the bit players on the periphery, involved, but scarcely capable of having played major roles—Penny Lincoln, Sid Thomas, yes, and include old Ben Hart on whose property the second dead man, Glenn Ronson, had been found. Each in his way, including Ronson himself, was an entity, standing out against the backdrop of Santo Cristo because of events, if not traits of personality.

Sid Thomas, of course, was a character in his own right, but important to the puzzle, as far as Johnny could see, only because of what he could reveal of Charley Harrington and Charley's attitudes and views.

Penny Lincoln up to a certain point was important only for the same reason. As a person, she was not much—unformed, shallow, and without force. But her involvement with Grace Cathcart—and here that fleeting thought Johnny had experienced before flashed across the screen of his mind and quickly disappeared again—that involvement *could* have importance far beyond its immoral or hedonistic values.

Old Ben Hart, of course, *was* a force to be reckoned with if, indeed, he had played any part at all in the drama. Johnny had hunted with Ben, and seen the old man looking through his sights at a charging grizzly. There was no give in old Ben, none at all; the grizzly's head mounted over Ben's huge fireplace was testimony to that. Had Ben in any way actually *played* a part?

But, characters aside, where in all this was motive for murder? A tapped telephone could be an annoyance, Johnny was prepared to admit, or even worse, it could be a threat to whatever Cathcart might be involved in that had managed to attract sufficient Federal attention that it had eventually been brought to Congressman Mark Hawley's attention. That, of course, was a possibility, but it didn't quite fit because it in no way explained Glenn Ronson's murder by the same brutal, shotgun method.

And what of Whitney's allegations that Charley Harrington had from time to time tapped Cathcart for money? How did that fit in? And if there had indeed been a phone tap, why in the world had the child Charley Harrington made it in the first place? Why choose Cathcart if he merely wanted to tap a phone line to see how it was done?

Forget for the moment Charley Harrington's death. Why was Glenn Ronson also killed? Was there a connection beyond the similarity of execution? Ronson's keys were missing. Was that the reason, in order to gain easy access to the Cathcart house for which Ronson was house-sitting? Then if access was important enough for murder, why was nothing taken during the break-in?

He had reached headquarters, and he walked automatically down the short hallway to his own office, seemingly random thoughts still running free in his mind.

Tony Lopez was waiting, and his face was unnaturally solemn. "Another phone call, *amigo*," Tony said in a quiet voice. "It was"—he hesitated over the name—"Enright. She sounded a little uptight. Here." Tony held out a slip of paper. "You're to call that number."

Johnny sat down, the random thoughts immediately wiped from his mind. "You talked with her?" he said.

Tony merely nodded.

"And she said what?"

"Just to call her back. That number."

There was something in Tony's voice that said more than the words. Johnny said, "Did you call the number?"

"*Sí.* I wanted to see if it was the hotel."

"Was it?"

"No." Tony hesitated. "So I hung up."

Johnny reached for the telephone. He punched the

123

keys savagely. Mark Hawley's voice answered. "A phone call from Cassie," Johnny said. He was looking at the written number now, his face set and strained. "Mexico City, I think. Do you have a way of finding whose number it is before I call it?"

There was a moment's silence. "You're expecting—problems, son?"

"You know better than I do. I asked you once if she was in any danger. If she is, we want to know where I'm calling before I call."

"I can see that." The congressman's voice was doubtful.

"But what?"

The hesitation was longer this time. "It's just that cooperation from the Mexico authorities is sometimes . . . less dependable than it might be. One of our narcotics agents, undercover, was—"

"Tortured and killed," Johnny said, biting off the words. "I know." Then, in a different tone, "Just what in hell have you let Cassie in for, Congressman?"

"Five minutes," the congressman said. "I'll call you back."

Johnny hung up. Tony watched him in silence. All at once Johnny pushed back his chair and sprang up. He turned toward the doorway.

Tony said gently, "Mexico City is a long way, *amigo.* You could get there, but when?" What he saw in Johnny's face then was frightening, and he wanted to look away, but he made himself hold his eyes steady.

Johnny took a long, deep breath. Slowly he nodded. "You're right." He sat down again and stared fixedly at the phone.

The call came within the five minutes. The congressman said, "We can try to trace the call. They think that's better than trying to run down the number first. Don't dial it. Put it through the long-distance operator. Trust me, son."

Johnny's face was carved in stone, an angry mask.

"You hear me?" the congressman said, sharper than before.

"I hear you." The words came out slowly, under pressure.

"Call her now. They're standing by."

Wordlessly, Johnny broke the connection, listened for the dial tone, and punched the *0* button. When the operator came on he said, spacing the words slowly, with effort, "I want to make a call to Mexico. Here is the number. . . ."

It seemed an eternity. There were multiple clicks on the line, and voices speaking in both English and Spanish. Johnny endured it all. At last there was the welcome sound of ringing. A voice said, "Yes?"

"Chica." The word was difficult to speak. *"Chica—"*

"I'm here." Cassie's voice was not distinct, as if she held the phone a distance from her mouth.

"Where are you?"

In the background a voice spoke rapid, muffled Spanish, the words all but indistinguishable. "I can't say," Cassie said.

"You can't say because you don't know, or because—"

Again the voice broke in, speaking rapidly, the words recognizable as Spanish only because of their rhythm. "I—can't say," Cassie said.

"Okay." Johnny's voice was soft, under tight control. "What do they want?"

"Nobody has told me."

Was there something behind the words? A message of some kind? "Is *he* there?" Johnny said, not wanting to mention Cathcart's name aloud.

"No." There was a pause. "Not yet."

"When you see him," Johnny said, "tell him—"

"No, señor," the background voice broke in, speaking Spanish. "We will tell him, as we are telling you. No more nonsense. Understood? Or both he *and* this one—" The voice broke off. "No matter. We will settle it our way."

"If you—" Johnny began, but with a decisive click the line went dead.

Johnny put the phone in its cradle very gently and just sat, staring at it. From the doorway Tony watched in silence. The office was very still.

"She can't say where she is," Johnny said in an uninflected, almost mechanical tone as if he were repeating a required lesson. "They will settle it their way." He looked up at Tony then, his eyes and moving lips the only alive things in the mask of his face. "What does that mean?"

Tony's shrug included his entire body and spread, upturned hands. He shook his head. "I don't know." He spoke in Spanish without knowing it.

"Tampoco," Johnny said. "Neither do I." His voice was no longer mechanical. It was soft, under careful control. "But when I do—"

The telephone rang and Johnny snatched it up. The congressman's voice said, "Did you find out anything?"

"No."

"They managed to trace the number."

"It won't do any good," Johnny said. "You know

126

that as well as I do. When they get there, *if* they get there, there won't be anybody."

"You may be right, son." The congressman's voice was quiet, thoughtful. "So what do you think we do now?"

"We wait," Johnny said. "What else?"

Lucille Harrington preferred to prowl while she thought. Waldo did his best thinking sitting quite still, staring at his desktop as at a chessboard. Neither looked at the other as they spoke, but their minds seemed to mesh harmoniously, not infrequently indulging in quantum leaps of deduction.

"Mr. Clancy at the bank," Lucille said thoughtfully as she picked a small Eskimo-carved soapstone walrus from a tabletop, appeared to study it, and then set it down again, "is quite sure that Charley received funds whose source has never been explained. Is that not correct?"

Waldo accepted the statement without comment and jumped forward from there. "The Cathcart telephone was allegedly tapped," he said. "We ought to be able to ascertain beyond doubt whether it was or not."

"Pursue that line," Lucille said. She ran her fingers

gently over the heads of three flammulated owls sculptured in bronze. "The possibilities are many."

"Charley could have been privy to Cathcart's trading practices, for one," Waldo said promptly.

"Or his precise financial transactions for another." This was Lucille.

"His comings and goings and a list of those he spoke with," Waldo said.

Lucille did not pause in her walking, but her mind took off in another direction. "Charley set up a dummy corporation via computer once," she said. "He could probably have done it again without much trouble."

"I am not intimately acquainted with the matter of accountability in the movement of money," Waldo said, following that line of thought, "but I was under the impression that large sums do come under a certain amount of scrutiny. And I believe we are talking about substantial amounts."

"One gathers from the newspapers," Lucille said, "that one of the government agencies, I believe it is the IRS, worries constantly about unreported income. It must follow that there is a great deal of it."

Waldo thought about it. "'Laundered money' is a phrase that keeps appearing. Are we talking about criminal activities?"

"Such as?"

"'Organized crime' is another phrase that pops up—illegal gambling, drugs, prostitution, various kinds of extortion. I assume that the 'laundering' of money is in order to avoid proof of those activities."

"Yes." Lucille's tone was definite. "The paperback mysteries I read often deal with such things. Swiss bank accounts seem to figure heavily—numbered,

rather than being listed under names, I understand."
She was silent for a few moments, continuing her slow pacing around the room. "If Charley could tap into the Lab's computer data—" she began.

"And," Waldo said, "via his computer obtain the bank's—would it be called password?"

"Then," Lucille said, "why could he not have obtained the number of someone's Swiss bank account? And would the number be all that is necessary for the transfer of funds? But to whom, without leaving a clear trail?" She stopped her walking then and turned to look at Waldo. He too was looking up from his imaginary chess game.

"A spurious dummy corporation," they said simultaneously.

"Which," Lucille went on smoothly, "would simply disappear once the funds had been disbursed."

"Purely hypothetical," Waldo said, "but it does bear investigation."

Lucille had resumed her prowling. "Who would be in a position to know about such things?"

Waldo studied the desktop again. "I have no idea."

Lucille was silent for a time. She said at last, "We have contributed to Congressman Hawley's campaigns. Why is he not a starting point? He does appear to know his way through the labyrinths of Washington. And he must be in the telephone directory."

Waldo already had the telephone book open. "Federal Office Building," he read. "I wasn't even aware that we had one." He dialed swiftly, and when a female voice answered, "My name is Waldo Harrington," he said. "I should like to speak with the congressman."

Mark Hawley came on the line at once. The name

Harrington touched a chord. "We've met, I think," he said. "And you are campaign contributors as well as constituents. What can I do for you?" He listened quietly, and when Waldo was done, "I think I'd like to hear more about that idea," the congressman said. "Where, and when?"

Waiting can be difficult. Johnny had never quite realized that before. All his life he had cultivated patience, which meant the ability to wait endlessly, apparently unaffected by the passage of time. But this was different. This concerned Cassie, which put the situation in a class entirely by itself.

Tony Lopez, worried, said, "Go for a walk, *amigo*. Anything happens, I'll find you."

Johnny was not interested in walking. Or in thinking. For the first time in his life he felt that if he did not *do* something, he would explode. He looked up sharply. "What was that you said?"

Tony felt almost pinned back against the wall by the ferocity of the question, but he made himself stand firm. "Cathcart's in Mexico City," he said.

"I know where Cathcart is. So?"

"He owns the Johnson Gallery."

"I know that too. What are you trying to get at?"

Tony lifted his shoulders in a massive shrug, and let them fall again. "I don't know, except that like I said, Johnson Gallery doesn't handle local artists or sculptors much. They get most of their things from out of the country—Mexico, especially. Maybe Cathcart's down there because—"

Johnny closed his eyes and thought rude thoughts about himself. He opened his eyes again, and when he spoke, his voice had lost much of its ferocity. "Sometimes," he said, "you make a great deal of sense, did you know that? And sometimes I am *estúpido!"* He pushed back his chair and stood up. "I'll be at the Johnson Gallery."

"But, of course," Tony said. He was tempted to show the white teeth in a wide smile, but decided it would be better not. "I will be here."

The Johnson Gallery was housed in its own one-story, expensive, and expensively decorated adobe building with a flagstoned pathway entrance along which Mexican clay planters filled with colorful potted chrysanthemums were regularly replenished by one of the local nurseries. The inside floor of the gallery was brick, dully polished, and the walls were painted in a subtle, off-white shade that would complement any kind or color of artwork.

Only a handful of paintings were hung, each having and deserving its own considerable space, and here and there statuary, both bronze and stone and mostly large-sized, stood on polished wooden tables or pedestals. It was not a gallery, Johnny reflected, where the average *turista* would feel welcome or at ease. No prices were shown; none were needed to indicate that what was for sale was expensive.

The strikingly attractive young woman who came out to meet him in the gallery's main room wore a long, full skirt, polished boots, and a voluminous overblouse contained at her slim waist by a silver-and-turquoise *concho* belt. Her eyes were dark, her skin faintly pigmented, and her glossy black hair drawn back severely. Vaguely familiar, Johnny thought, and searched his memory file. Of course, of course. "Monica Jaramillo," he said, "no?"

"That is correct, Lieutenant." She did not smile. "Is there something I can do for you?"

"I don't know yet." Simple truth. Johnny looked around at the statuary. There was what had to be the nude Cassie had mentioned. The depicted body was sexually attractive, but it held nothing for Johnny. His eyes went on, to a guitar player, an Aztec head in stone, a bronze *caballero* gracefully controlling a rearing horse, and across the room a massive, crouching jaguar showing tension in every sleek muscled line.

Johnny's eyes swept on, taking in the paintings on the walls, and returned seemingly of their own volition to the jaguar at which he stared for a moment or two, puzzled by an incongruity he could not immediately identify. Monica Jaramillo watched him quietly.

"That jaguar," Johnny said at last.

"What about it, Lieutenant?"

"Bronze," Johnny said. He had learned about such things from Cassie. "It must be heavy for such a fragile-looking pedestal."

"It is not heavy, Lieutenant. It is bronze powder in polymer, hollow, and for its size quite light." She seemed to be waiting for Johnny's next question; her dark eyes watched his steadily and with a certain boldness.

"Are you still married?" Johnny said.

"No, *señor*. I was—divorced eighteen months ago."

"He, Roberto, is still in prison?"

"That is correct, Lieutenant. Where you put him."

"Where he put himself," Johnny said.

The woman shrugged. "As you wish, *señor*. We are no longer married, so it is all one to me."

Johnny gestured around the room. "Do you carry any local artists?"

"Very few. The *patrón* is a great admirer of Mexican art."

"Ross Cathcart."

"That is correct. It is no secret, Lieutenant."

Something was scurrying around in the edges of Johnny's mind like a mouse half-seen in the shadows of a room, and he tried and failed to identify it. No matter; in due time it would show itself. In the meantime, "Jaramillo is your maiden name, no?" he said.

"It is, Lieutenant."

"A proud name here in New Mexico."

The woman inclined her head in faint acknowledgment.

"Your—husband's name, I believe, is Lewis?"

She faced him squarely. "We were not legally married, *señor*. I believe you were quite aware of that."

"I like to have things straight."

Again the faint nod of acknowledgment. "Understood. Do you have other questions?"

Johnny was looking around again at the other bronze sculptures. "Are these too—what was it you said?—bronze powder in polymer, also hollow, also light?"

"The nude is solid bronze. The guitar player and the *caballero* on horseback are bronze powder and polymer. Is that important, Lieutenant? You are an art critic?"

Johnny shook his head. "Just interested." He could not have said why.

"Because you like to have things straight, is that it?" Her tone was cool, faintly scornful.

As Johnny drove back to his office, wondering what, if anything, he had accomplished or found out, it occurred to him that Monica Jaramillo and Grace Cathcart were in many ways quite similar—both stunningly attractive, strong, self-possessed, and not easily shaken. He wondered why that thought had come to mind. No matter. He was thinking again of Cassie, who was a very different article indeed, although in her own way equally strong.

Tony Lopez met him in the hallway. "Visitors," Tony said. "The Harringtons." He hesitated. "And Congressman Hawley called." Tony's eyes were suddenly sad. "The Mexico City telephone they called from is located in a deserted office. It had not yet been disconnected." He shook his head. "No one had seen anyone."

As he had anticipated, Johnny thought, and made himself contain the anger he felt. He walked into his office where Lucille and Waldo Harrington waited and sat down at his desk.

Lucille said, "We have just come from Mark Hawley."

Johnny's expression tightened. He said nothing.

"We had a theory about Charley's unaccounted-for funds," Waldo said. "The congressman was interested."

"Maybe I am too," Johnny said, and made himself listen carefully while Lucille explained their thinking concerning a numbered Swiss bank account and a spurious nonexistent corporation which could disappear once purloined funds had been received. Despite thoughts of Cassie, Johnny was impressed by the ingenuity of the Harrington's thinking, and said so.

"Pure hypothesis, of course," Lucille said, and

135

again Johnny was impressed by her calmness as she spoke of her dead son. "But Charley was ingenious, and we find the possibility consistent with his some-times tortuous thinking. The congressman may have ways of checking the theory out."

"Mark Hawley," Johnny said, thinking again of course of Cassie, "has all kinds of ways and means he can use, and he knows how to use them."

Lucille studied him quietly. "You seem upset," she said. "At us?"

Johnny shook his head. He produced a sheepish smile which, on his usually harsh face, was totally incongruous. "No way. A different thing entirely. Was that all you wanted to tell me?"

"Not quite," Waldo said, glanced at Lucille, who nodded, and then produced Charley Harrington's letter that had been left in his safe box addressed to them. Waldo explained the circumstances. "We felt," Waldo said, "that perhaps parts of the letter might be of interest to you. May I read you the pertinent passages?"

Johnny glanced at Lucille's face as he nodded. She was holding herself under tight control, he thought admiringly, and, trying to emulate her, pushed thoughts of Cassie from his mind as he listened to Charley Harrington's words concerning anticipation of his own death.

Waldo finished reading, and Lucille said in a voice that sounded quite normal, "Nothing specific, I am afraid, but we thought—" Her sudden smile was sad, and turned inward upon her own thoughts and feel-ings. "Perhaps I should say we—hoped that it might be of help."

"It sheds some light," Johnny said as gently as he

136

could, "and in the end it may be of considerable help." How, he had no idea, but—

Lucille said, "There is one more part, a small, and perhaps entirely extraneous part—" She held out her hand for the letter.

Waldo, frowning, gave it to her. "I don't believe I follow," he began, and then slowly nodded and relaxed in his chair. "Of course," he said, "of course. I overlooked the possible implications."

"The last paragraph," Lucille said, "deals with another matter entirely. It reads, 'Lastly, I ask a personal favor which I hope you will not find too onerous. There is a girl named Penelope Lincoln—' I will skip his comments concerning her, and come to the point. '. . . I have enjoyed the company of Penny the person, and I hope and trust that our association has not placed her in any jeopardy. If it turns out that it has, I ask that you do what you can to help her.'" Eyes averted, Lucille finished reading, folded the letter carefully, and handed it back to Waldo. Then, at last she looked again at Johnny. "Do you know this young person?" she said.

"I've talked with her." Johnny's face was expressionless. Penny Lincoln and Charley Harrington, he was thinking; Penny Lincoln and Grace Cathcart; Grace Cathcart and her husband—again things only half-seen were scurrying around the edges of his mind.

"What kind of person is she?" Lucille said suddenly. "I mean—" She stopped and shook her head slowly. "I apologize. I am behaving like an hysterical parent. It is ridiculous."

But understandable, Johnny thought, and was tempted to say so, but refrained. "She is an artist."

Lucille nodded. "So Charley says. And not a very good one."

Sam's assessment too, Johnny thought, but said only, "I haven't seen any of her work, and wouldn't be competent to judge it if I had."

Lucille still watched him steadily.

"You didn't ask what she did," Johnny said. "You asked what kind of a person she is." He nodded, and thought again of Sam's assessment. "I'm afraid she's young, and a little . . . mixed-up. She hasn't sorted things out yet." And probably never will, he thought, but said no more.

Lucille stood up. She held out her hand. "Thank you for your consideration," she said. Her voice changed, softened. "I find you a kinder man than I would have thought."

"Keep in touch," Johnny said. "And if you have any more ideas—"

"We will bring them to you." Lucille was smiling now, composure restored. *"Adiós."* And, the smile spreading, she added, "Johnny."

Tony Lopez walked in as the Harringtons went down the hall.

"You heard?" Johnny said, and watched Tony's nod. "So what do we have?" The question was rhetorical.

He had risen when Lucille had stood. He dropped back into his chair now, looked at the far wall, and spoke almost as if to himself. "Charley Harrington thought he might be killed. That explains the life insurance and naming them as beneficiaries. Or seems to. Penny Lincoln is something else. She—" He stopped. Again those half-hidden thoughts were scurrying around. "Why might Charley have thought she might be in jeopardy?" He looked at Tony.

Tony spread his hands and shrugged. "You tell me, *amigo.*"

Johnny was silent, staring hard at the wall again. "If Cassie were here—" he began, and there he stopped because the thought of Cassie's not being here, but being somewhere out of reach and possibly in danger of some kind was almost unbearable.

He pushed back his chair and stood up, finding inactivity impossible. "A walk," he said, and then shook his head at a sudden thought. "No. I'll be up at Flora Hobbs's place." He glared at Tony.

"I was not smirking," Tony said, and then did show the white teeth in a broad grin. "I will not smirk until you have gone."

Flora was at home. She showed Johnny into her quiet office and closed the door. "Sit down. A drink?" She was wise in the ways of men, and this man, she saw, was sorely troubled.

Johnny sat down and shook his head. He made himself relax. There was nothing he could do about Cassie, he told himself, and futile rage accomplished nothing. For long moments he was silent, concentrating on and absorbing the sights and the sounds around him.

Through large, translucently curtained windows he could see the inner courtyard with its neat, carefully raked, graveled paths, its beds of flowers—now in October, chrysanthemums, as at the Johnson Gallery —and vaguely hear the splashing fountain, a cool sound, always welcome in this arid land. He felt vaguely soothed.

Flora was sitting behind her desk, watching him quietly.

"Two women," Johnny said at last, "lovers, would they—talk much?" He was conscious of the outrageousness of the question, but he hoped that Flora, in her knowledge and wisdom, might see through the surface tactlessness.

Flora was unable to control herself. She smiled faintly, but without mockery. "Before," she said, "during, or afterwards?"

"I would guess—afterwards." Johnny felt no embarrassment at discussing the subject, in a sense dissecting it, with a woman. He was concentrating on pursuit of an unknown quarry, and as in a hunt when the tracks led through strange country he was oblivious to all else.

Flora said, "I should think talk was possible." She paused. "Perhaps even likely."

"Just idle talk? Like they had met at the market? Or could it be—" Johnny, unable to find a word, spread his hands.

"Intimate?" Flora said. She nodded. "Perhaps."

"Sometimes men," Johnny said slowly, "tell their women things they wouldn't tell anyone else."

Flora smiled again. "Yes."

"Might it be—the same with two women?"

"I see what you mean." Flora thought about it. "I should think it might well be. Under certain circumstances."

"One woman dominant," Johnny said. "The other—" Again he spread his hands. "Younger, not sure of herself, just . . . going along with what came."

"You paint quite a picture," Flora said. "Representational, not abstract. What you describe is not un-common."

"Which way would the conversation most likely go?"

Flora was silent for a time. She said at last, "Both ways, I should think, but the two ways would be different."

"Explain that."

"You ask hard questions, Johnny."

Johnny sat silent, waiting.

"The submissive woman," Flora said, "would want reassurance, praise, flattery, anything to bolster her uncertainty. She might tend to—ask questions, I should think, hoping for flattering answers."

"And the other?"

"Probably happily relaxed. She might talk about whatever happened to be in her mind, because she wouldn't need reassurance or flattery. Oh, she would enjoy adulation." Again the smile. "Most women do. But it would not be essential. Her talk would be more her . . . own thinking." Flora paused again. "Is that what you wanted?"

Johnny stood up. "Yes," he said. "Thanks."

Flora's smile this time was real and amused. "Now would you like that drink?"

Johnny shook his head. "Thanks. I'll be on my way." He was gone.

12

Johnny was at home that night, sitting staring into the piñon fire, Chico at his feet, when the telephone call came. Cassie's voice, a trifle unsteady, said only, "I'm in San Antonio. Ross Cathcart is with me. We will land at Albuquerque at ten twenty-eight and I will be home within the hour. Don't meet me, please. I have my car."

"Chica—"

"All right?" Cassie said.

Johnny hesitated momentarily. Then, "If you say so," he said, and immediately the telephone went dead.

He hung up slowly and walked back to stare again at the fire. He had no idea what Cassie had been trying to tell him between the lines, nor was there any way he saw that he could find out, but the unmistakable thrust of her message was plain: "It is mandatory that you stay away." Why?

He sat down again, and his hand went automatically to Chico's ears and began to rub them gently. Cassie was back in the States, and by that much the situation had improved. But why was she with Cathcart, and why the—mystery? For a long time he sat quiet, his face showing nothing and his hand moving automatically, rhythmically on the dog's ears and head while his mind walked slowly around the puzzle, examining it from all sides before it reached a decision.

At last he stood up and walked again to the phone, dialed a number he had in his personal directory. Congressman Mark Hawley answered sleepily on the first ring.

"Cassie just called from San Antonio," Johnny said. "She's on her way home. With Cathcart. She arrives at Albuquerque at ten twenty-eight and she doesn't want me there. That was the entire conversation."

The congressman said, "You've figured out why? You wouldn't have called me else."

"Just a guess." The harsh lines in Johnny's face were very plain now. "There's somebody else flying with them who doesn't want to be seen by me. That's all I can come up with."

"Sounds like pretty good thinking to me," the congressman said. He was silent a moment. "I could arrange to shake down everybody on the flight—"

"No. That would be as bad as me being there."

"Maybe you're right, son. She's coming home, you say? Then when she gets there she can tell you who—"

"I doubt if she knows who it is. It makes no sense otherwise."

"I'm beginning to think straight again, son," the congressman said. "You got into this because of Cassie. You're getting her back. Well and good. Leave it there. With me."

Johnny shook his head angrily and opened his mouth to protest, but the phone went dead in his ear, and after a long, hesitant moment, he hung up, left the phone, and went back to drop down on the sofa and sit staring into the fire again. Chico lay down and rested his chin on Johnny's foot; he rolled his eyes upward to see if he could fathom his person's mood.

Nine, nine-thirty, ten, ten-thirty—the time seemed endless. By now, Cassie should be at the airport in Albuquerque. Would she drive up with Cathcart? No, Cathcart would have his own car. Or perhaps Grace Cathcart would be meeting him. Either way, Cassie would be coming home alone. Johnny tried not to look at his watch as the minutes continued to tick by.

Would there be someone following her? No. Where she lived, and with whom was no secret. And it would be no problem to find out that she worked at the museum, either. So? So what it all added up to was that Cassie was—vulnerable, a sitting duck, target for person or persons unknown. But why? And that was worst of all, because unless some reason for all this appeared, there was no starting place, not even a direction to look. The feeling of utter helplessness was not something Johnny was used to. It filled his mind with a sense of near despair.

Chico heard the car first and raised his head from Johnny's foot. He trotted to the door, tail up, making small, whimpering sounds of eagerness. Johnny followed, opened the door, and stepped out into the night to wait as the headlights turned in, the car stopped, the lights and engine were switched off, and as the door opened the dome light silhouetted Cassie unmistakably as she stepped out of the car.

"Chica—" Johnny was astonished to find that even the single word was difficult to get out.

"I'm here. I'm all right." Cassie's voice too was more than a little breathless. Then, the words coming out in a rush, "Hold me, Johnny. I'm still scared!"

They sat for a long time on the sofa facing the piñon fire, which crackled gently and gave off its familiar fragrance. Chico's head rested on Johnny's foot, his rump on Cassie's.

"You don't know who," Johnny said, summing up their conversation so far. "How many other passengers were there?"

"The plane was full. And we were in first class. I've never been in first class before. The curtain to the tourist section was closed, so—"

"Could he have been with you in first class?" Johnny shook his head angrily. "Or they? And we don't even know if it's man or woman."

"I don't think so. I can't be sure."

"All right. At baggage claim—"

"All I had was one carry-on case. The small one. So I didn't go to baggage claim. I went straight outside and took the shuttle to my car."

"You weren't followed?"

"I don't think so. Does it matter?"

"Probably not. In Mexico City when you were taken—"

"It was a taxi. I was going to meet Ross Cathcart for

145

dinner, as I told you. I got in the taxi and a man got in right behind me. He had a gun. At least he seemed to. In his coat pocket. He told the driver where to go."

"An office building."

"Yes. How did you—?"

"Mark Hawley. Not that it matters. Would you recognize the man?"

"Yes. But I never saw him again. He took me to the office and then he went away. The others—"

"How many?"

"Three. And Ross Cathcart, who came in after I did."

"You could recognize the three?"

"Yes."

"None of them was on the plane?"

"No. I looked at everybody as best I could. They weren't there."

"What did they say? To you? To Cathcart?"

"They didn't say anything to him. I think he had already been—talked to, told. He tried not to look frightened, but he was. And he was a little rumpled as if they had—" Cassie stopped and took a deep breath. "I don't know what had happened, but he, Ross Cathcart, was very quiet, subdued." She shook her head. "Not like himself."

"Did they rough you up at all?"

"Nobody touched me, Johnny. I thought—" Again she stopped and shook her head. "I was afraid, but nothing happened."

"All right, *chica*. Easy. What did they tell you?"

"To call you."

"That was all?"

Cassie nodded silently. "I got Tony Lopez."

"Yes."

"The rest you know. You heard them—him on the phone."

Johnny nodded shortly. "And then?"

"The hotel. For my things. Then the airport."

"Three men?"

"Only one. And Cathcart. That—man did have a gun. I saw it. He showed it to us." Cassie took a deep, unsteady breath. "He would have used it, Johnny. I knew that."

"Yes," Johnny said. "I can believe it." The lines of his face were very harsh. "And at the airport?"

"He gave us the tickets. He told us we would be—watched. He told me to call you from San Antonio."

"And tell me what? Exactly what?"

"That I was coming, and when, but not to meet me. He made that plain."

Johnny stared at the fire in silence. "So," he said slowly, "he, they wanted somebody to meet the plane, but not me."

"I—don't understand. Why do you think that?"

"Why else would he have told you to tell me your arrival time?"

"Oh."

"So either my phone is tapped—" Johnny shook his head. "That I doubt." He looked at Cassie then. "Or somebody was listening when you called and talked to me. Where did you call from?"

"There is a bank of phones. I used one of them." Cassie closed her eyes remembering. "I wasn't the only one making a call." She looked at Johnny. "You know how it is at an airport. People are always making telephone calls."

Johnny nodded. "Was Cathcart with you? Could he

have heard?" He shook his head. "Doesn't matter. He knew as well as you did when your plane was due in Albuquerque."

"He wasn't with me. He—" Cassie almost giggled. "He couldn't wait to get—to—the—toilet even though he had already been twice on the plane! He was still there—"

The telephone rang, and Johnny jumped up from the sofa and crossed the room in two long steps. "Yes?" he said into the phone. His tone was hard.

"Mark Hawley here, son. She's home safe?"

"She's home."

"Good. Drop by my office first thing in the morning, son."

"What—?"

"See you then," the congressman said, and hung up.

Johnny walked slowly back to the sofa. Cassie was watching him. Her face was anxious. "Mark Hawley wants to see me," Johnny said. "I'm not sure, but maybe I can guess why." His tone changed, and he managed a smile. "It's been a long day, *chica*. Let's call it quits and go to bed." He held both hands out to help her up.

Cassie took them and rose to her feet. She was smiling unsteadily. "I think," she said slowly, "that that's the best thing anyone has said to me all day."

Breakfast was a quiet time. Cassie was still subdued, but no longer jumpy. "It's—hard to explain," she said at last over a second cup of coffee, "but they—all of them—were unlike anyone I had ever met before. They—"

"Mexicans? All of them?"

Cassie shook her head doubtfully. *"Latinos,"* she

said, "but—Mexican? I can't say. They all spoke Spanish. Cathcart does too, did you know that?"

"Yes. Tony Lopez told me. Go on."

"They—" She stopped and shivered faintly. "Implacable is the word. Merciless. They would have no—hesitation in doing anything." Her eyes searched Johnny's for reaction. "Do you know what I mean?"

"I can believe it."

"Do you know—?"

"Only guesswork so far, *chica*. I don't *know* anything. Yet." He pushed back his chair and stood up, carried plate and coffee cup to the sink, rinsed them thoroughly, his back to Cassie, his motions almost angry-seeming. "Maybe Mark Hawley will shed some light." He started for the door and stopped, turned. "I don't think you need to worry now, *chica*. Don't try to look in every direction at once. It won't do any good. Nobody's going to bother you. Not up here."

Cassie nodded silently.

"Believe me," Johnny said.

She could smile faintly then. "I'll try." And then, quickly, "I—made a mess of things, didn't I? I'm sorry. I thought I could help."

"You did fine, *chica*. You may have flushed something out of the chamisa." His face changed, hardened. "But next time—"

"I will behave," Cassie said. "That is a promise."

Johnny nodded shortly and was gone.

Mark Hawley said, "Sit down, son. How's Cassie?"

"She'll be all right."

The congressman nodded. "She's resilient, that one. But I'm sorry she had to go through what she did." He picked a bulky folder from his desktop and held it out. "Here. Look through these. See if you recognize anyone."

They were glossy, eight-by-ten, black-and-white photos, sharp and clear, obviously enlarged to show plainly every facial detail. "Everyone aboard that plane from San Antonio," Mark Hawley said, "including the crew. Cassie and Cathcart are in the batch too."

Johnny went through the pictures one by one, without haste, and when he was through stacked them in a neat pile and shook his head. "Nobody I know. Except Cassie and Cathcart, of course."

"Sure?" The congressman smiled. "Yes, you would be, son. All right. It was just a chance."

"You've checked names?"

"All of them. Some had passports, most didn't. They aren't really required. Name-check turned up nothing."

Johnny riffled through the pile again. "Not even a pattern I can see. Some I'd say are Hispanic—"

"And some of those are U.S. citizens. You're right. It's a mixed batch."

Johnny said, "Who met the plane?"

The congressman took his time to walk around his desk and sit down. "Dwell on that, son."

"If Cassie was overheard calling me from San Antonio, which is the only way the phone call makes sense, then whoever heard the arrival time could have called it ahead to have someone meet the plane, no?"

The congressman thought about it and nodded slowly. "It makes just as much sense as somebody actually flying with them. Yes. That means—"

"So maybe," Johnny said, "it means we've got at

least a piece of an organization right here in Santo Cristo under our noses. My nose." His face was suddenly angry.

Mark Hawley said mildly, "You're making a big, blind guess about Cathcart, aren't you, son?"

"Am I? I don't think it's much of a guess. Cathcart's a commodities trader who dabbles occasionally in stocks. There's nothing there that would tend to bring out men with guns in Mexico City." He was ticking off points on his fingers as he talked. "He owns and apparently runs an art gallery that specializes in Mexican art. But what's there to produce threat of violence? We're not talking about something by Van Gogh worth multimillion bucks. This artwork is big, and obvious, and right out where you can look at it." He ticked off another finger. "So?"

"Go on," the congressman said.

"So what are we talking about?" Johnny said. "Something that means organization or the Mexico City business wouldn't have been handled the way it was. That means big bucks. It's also something you don't want me messing into. That means it's Fed business. What does that add up to but dope coming through here, probably headed for California?"

The congressman wore his poker face. "No comment."

"Okay." Johnny stood up. "But I'm interested in Cathcart for another reason, and that is because everywhere I look I find him tied somehow to Charley Harrington. And Charley Harrington and Glenn Ronson are my business."

The congressman sighed. "I'll give you that, son." He heaved himself out of his chair. "Maybe a mite early for a drink," he said, "but I didn't get much sleep last night and a little sip of bourbon might help. Join me?"

"No, thanks." Johnny made himself relax, and even smiled faintly. "Nothing personal. Just, like you say, a little early in the day." He paused. "May I borrow those photos?"

"Mind telling me why?"

"Tony Lopez. He's related to half of Santo Cristo and pretty well knows the other half. He may see a face he recognizes."

The congressman was already at his cupboard, pouring a shot of whiskey. "Help yourself, son. Help yourself." His voice sharpened. "But keep in touch, hear?"

"It seems to be a one-way street," Johnny said, "but I'll do it."

Tony Lopez went through the photos and then, as Johnny had, stacked them neatly and put them back in the folder. "Three faces I recognize," he said, and shook his head. "Cathcart, Dr. Enright, and Pablo Gonzalez—"

"Who's he?"

"Grew up here in Santo Cristo," Tony said. "Lives in Albuquerque now. Has a shop that sells Mexican pottery, cheap *serapes,* that kind of thing." He shook his head again, showing the white teeth in a broad smile. "Include him out, *amigo.* He's harmless."

"How do you know?"

It hardly seemed possible, but the smile spread even farther. "We used to call him *conejo.* And that still fits him. Rabbit Gonzalez. Scared of his own shadow. Show him a gun or a knife and he'd faint."

It was, Johnny reflected, precisely the kind of dead end you ran into again and again and again.

"So now what?" Tony said.

Johnny got up from his desk. "I think I'll have another talk with Cathcart. Cassie said he was a little shaken up. Maybe he'll talk a bit more this time."

13

Grace Cathcart answered the door. This morning she wore tailored frontier trousers, a silk blouse, and polished boots instead of the blue silk robe Johnny had last seen her in, but her face, her eyes, and her manner were no more friendly. "Yes, Lieutenant?"

"I'd like to see your husband."

"He is tired, Lieutenant. He just returned last night from Mexico City. It was an—exhausting trip."

"I know all about it. That's why I want to see him."

"Lieutenant—"

"Now," Johnny said, allowing an edge to appear in his voice. "Among other things, I'm investigating two murders, and if I have to get a warrant and have him brought down to my office—"

"Wait here," Grace Cathcart said, and closed the door. She was gone only a matter of moments. "My husband will see you," she said, and led the way into what seemed to be Cathcart's study. It was empty. "He'll be with you in a moment," Grace Cathcart said, and walked out, her slim back straight and resentful.

Johnny looked around. There were paintings on the walls, mostly oils, but here and there a watercolor. The subjects were diverse, but most were unmistakably *latino,* and all bore the same expensive look he had seen at the gallery.

On a library table behind the large, heavy, carved desk was a computer. Its screen was dark. *Probably hooked into a stock-and/or-commodity price-quotes service,* Johnny thought. On the desk itself were three telephones, and Johnny looked at them and wondered idly which one Charley Harrington was supposed to have tapped. Or perhaps all three? And maybe the computer as well? From what Johnny had heard of the boy, very little would have been beyond him.

From the doorway Cathcart said, "What is it this time, Lieutenant?"

Johnny turned to study the man. He was dressed this morning in tan twill trousers, polished loafers, and a polo shirt. He was clean-shaven, and his eyes did not look bleary from lack of sleep. He looked, in fact, Johnny thought, quite alert and self-possessed. If Cassie's assessment of Cathcart's nervousness had been correct—and Johnny would have been willing to bet that it was—then the man had pulled himself together well.

"Business in Mexico City?" Johnny said mildly.

"That, Lieutenant, is no concern of yours."

"Maybe up to a point. Beyond that, it's very much

my business." He took his time to study Cathcart's face, and then quite deliberately sat down in a leather club chair.

"Make yourself at home," Cathcart said, sarcasm plain.

Johnny ignored the remark. His eyes had not left Cathcart's face, and his tone now was no longer idly conversational. "Let's start with the deserted office in Mexico City where the telephone call was made to me," he said.

"I know nothing about any telephone call."

"You came in after it was made? Because you were there when I called."

"Was I?"

"Amigo," Johnny said, switching to Spanish, "do not play games. I am in no mood for it. You came, or were brought to the office. You had been—roughed up a little. In good time I will find out why. And by whom. You were frightened. Aboard the plane you went to the toilet twice, and yet could hardly wait to get to the toilet again in the airport in San Antonio." He switched back to English. "Did you wet your pants?"

"I think," Cathcart said, "I have taken just about all that—"

"I haven't even begun yet," Johnny said. "Because of you a friend of mine was badly treated. I don't like that even a small bit. My friend was told to call me from San Antonio. She did and—"

Cathcart's resentment had disappeared. He was clearly unsure of himself now. "I wasn't present when she called you. If she called you."

"I know that. You were in the john again."

"Then—"

"Who met you at Albuquerque? Was waiting to meet you?"

Cathcart blinked.

Behind Johnny, Grace Cathcart said, "I met him. He had telephoned me. I drove him home."

Nothing changed in Johnny's face. "Fair enough." He turned again to Cathcart. "But who met you before your wife turned up?" He was guessing, but it almost had to be, and he allowed no doubts to show.

Cathcart hesitated and then shook his head. "No one met me."

"I can check," Johnny said. "And I will. There are always witnesses, people who notice things. If I have to I'll have pictures of you circulated and—"

"No one met me," Cathcart said again, but his eyes were uncertain; they were, Johnny thought, the eyes of a man trying to decide whether to stay in the pot with the cards he held, knowing that they were maybe not quite good enough. "But," Cathcart said, his mind apparently made up at last, "I did see someone I knew and we . . . exchanged a few words."

"Who was that?"

"My attorney. Who is also a friend. And I do not see that that concerns you—"

"I'll decide what concerns me," Johnny said. "I told you my interest in this is not only official, it's also personal. A very good friend was involved. You just happened to see your lawyer, you said, who is also a friend. Okay. Who is he?"

"Joseph Whitney. He is—"

"Whitney is your lawyer too?" Johnny's face was still expressionless, but in his mind he was trying to fit in this new information. It did not fit easily. "Since when?"

"Our association," Cathcart said, "goes back a long way. A very long way. And, as I said, I do not see how that concerns you in any way, Lieutenant."

Johnny stood up. "Maybe you're right," he said in a new, quieter tone. He could even smile. "It could be." He glanced at Grace Cathcart.

She was watching him closely, but she said nothing. "Yesterday when we talked—" Johnny began.

Grace Cathcart's face retained its smooth, distant expression as she said, "I have not told my husband that you insisted on seeing me yesterday, Lieutenant. I was afraid it might upset him."

"Damn it," Cathcart said, almost as if on cue. "It does! What right did you have to bother my wife behind my back?"

"Why," Johnny said, "the same right you had to ask Cassie Enright to dinner with the idea of taking her to bed afterward. You'd tried before. It wouldn't have worked this time, either."

In the silence he walked out before he said something he might later regret. He needed time to sort things out because they seemed to be getting more and more complicated.

Back at headquarters, to Tony Lopez who leaned against the wall, "So there we have it," Johnny said. "Whitney was Harrington's attorney. He has apparently also been Cathcart's for some time. I think we can believe Cathcart on that because it would be too easy to check. Two men, in a sense, adversaries, represented by the same counsel. Does that make sense?"

Tony's massive shrug was his only answer.

"And it was Whitney," Johnny added, "who came

to tell me—no, to hint that maybe Cathcart was not quite as innocent as he might seem. That's not the way you treat a client."

"You want to talk to Whitney?" Tony said. "You want me to get him?"

Johnny thought about it, and shook his head. "Not yet." He sat quiet for a little time. "Penny Lincoln," he said at last and looked up at Tony. "Do you know where her studio is? She won't be at Sam's yet. Too early."

Tony pushed himself away from the wall. That, at least, he could find out. He was back shortly. "Up Canyon Road. A compound belongs to Judge Roybal. Number five."

Johnny stood up. *"Gracias.* I'll be there."

Number five was a separate building in the compound, old adobe, with faded blue window frames and flanking the front door a pitiful attempt at a small flower garden—marigolds, dahlias, and snapdragons—now blackened by frost.

Johnny knocked on the door, waited, and knocked again. Penny Lincoln's voice called sleepily, "All right, all right! I'm coming!" And in a moment or two the girl appeared in a chenille robe, obviously just awakened. "Oh, it's you. What do you want?"

"A little talk." Johnny's tone was gentle. Like the garden, he thought, and despite her youth, the girl was somehow already beyond full bloom. Pity.

"Okay. Come in." The girl's voice was resigned. "Give me a minute, wash my face, brush my teeth anyway."

There were two rooms, Johnny saw, small, cramped, with a tiny kitchenette and, beyond the bedroom, apparently a bathroom where water ran, a toilet flushed, and from which shortly Penny emerged, still in the chenille robe.

An oil painting in process stood on an easel. Johnny glanced at it and looked away again.

"Not very good, is it?" Penny Lincoln said. "I know. I just kid myself sometimes that I can paint." She shook her head. "I can't, and I never will." The brittle cynicism appeared. "So what else is new?"

"You were with Grace Cathcart yesterday," Johnny said.

"Was I?" The girl's eyes held his briefly, and then fell away. "What of it?"

"I'm not trying to make anything of it," Johnny said, "except that you were there with her. You've been there before too, haven't you?" His tone was still gentle.

"What are you, some kind of morals freak?"

"No. Your morals don't bother me a bit, except—"

"There it is. Except what? You think I'm the only one in this town goes—both ways? You'd better think again, mister. There's—"

"I told you your morals don't bother me a bit." His tone was firmer now. "But I don't want them to get you into big trouble."

"What kind of trouble? With the law? That's a laugh. Here in this town—"

"Charley Harrington was murdered," Johnny said. "I'm not sure why. Yet. But it was maybe because he knew too much." He had the girl's attention now. Her eyes searched his face, blinking in surprise. "It could be that you know too much too."

"Me?" The girl shook her head emphatically. "You've got the wrong girl, mister. I—" She stopped. Her tongue appeared, moistened her lips, and disappeared quickly like a small, frightened animal. "What could I know about anything?"

"I don't know. But somebody may think you do."

"That's crazy! How—?"

Johnny said, his voice gentle again, "Do you and Grace Cathcart talk much?"

"I don't go there to talk."

"I understand that. But . . . afterward?"

Penny closed her eyes. The tip of her tongue appeared again, and again fled back into her mouth. She shook her head. "I don't know!" It was almost a wail. Her eyes were open again, and they searched Johnny's anxiously. "About what? I mean, sure, maybe, when it's all over, you know, you don't want to jump right up and split! I guess maybe we . . . talk some. Is there anything wrong with that?"

"Nothing at all. It's perfectly natural. What kind of things do you talk about?"

"What do you think?" The girl's voice was almost belligerent. "I mean, we just—you know—you don't need pictures, do you? Do you?"

"No," Johnny said, "I don't need pictures. Or diagrams."

"Well, then, okay! So what do we talk about? Was it good? Was it—what the hell can I say?"

"I mean other things," Johnny said. "Like your painting? Her trip to England and Scotland? The plays she saw in London? That kind of thing?"

"Oh." Penny was silent and her expression softened. "Well, sure, I guess sometimes we do. You feel—you know—good, relaxed. You just say whatever comes into your mind. You—" She stopped, and shook her head. "I guess you don't know how it is, do you? Not really." Again she was silent momentarily, thinking, remembering. "But guys talk too, you know?"

"I know," Johnny said. Came now the big question. "Did Charley Harrington talk much?"

Penny's expression changed swiftly. A tiny smile appeared. "He was—far out. Sometimes he talked, sure. But sometimes he didn't say a thing, just lay there, like—you know—"

"Listening? To you?"

The tiny smile spread as memory returned in a flood. "Yeah. Sometimes he made me feel—you know —like I was important, like what I said mattered!" She was silent again. The smile disappeared. "She— you know who—she never makes me feel like that. Funny, isn't it? The difference, I mean?"

The phone on Cassie's desk rang. She picked it up, spoke her name, and a voice said in rapid Spanish, "We know where to find you any time, day or night. Tell your policeman that. Tell him he should not have sent you to Mexico City to poke around. We do not like snoopers." The word in Spanish is *fisgónes;* it has myriad connotations. "Understood?" The line went dead.

Cassie hung up and sat quietly, remembering vividly with an almost sick feeling her fright in that deserted office after the taxi ride which had been in effect a kidnapping. As she had told Johnny, these were men like none she had encountered before; there was about them an air almost of indifference, as if whatever they might do—violent, brutal, even deadly —would to them have no real meaning beyond the results that might be obtained.

Somehow, and it still astonished her that the analogy had come to mind, she had found herself wondering if medieval torturers might have been more like this than like the sadistic monsters they were usually shown to be in films. And she had found this attitude of cold dispassion far more frightening than open threats.

Now, despite Johnny's assurance this morning, she was up against the same cold echo of implied violence, and she found it difficult to control her breathing or quiet the faint trembling in her hands.

From beneath her desk, Chico's head appeared. He looked up at her, trying to comprehend the sudden change of mood he sensed. He whimpered softly in question.

"It's all right," Cassie said softly. "All right." And she patted the dog's head. She could only hope that what she said was true, but her instincts told her that it was not.

Grace Cathcart, still in the frontier pants and polished boots, slim, self-possessed, but unmistakably feminine, came again into her husband's study that morning. Ross Cathcart was on one of the three telephones, and the computer screen behind him was lighted and filled with changing numbers and symbols. He frowned at his wife, said into the phone, "All right. That's it," and hung up. "I'm busy," he told Grace.

"So I see." She sat down, gracefully, as she did all things. "But I think it's time we had a talk."

"Damn it—"

"Don't bluster. It doesn't become you. It's as bad as the false passion you sometimes pretend. And as phony." She sat quietly, her eyes on his, her hands

163

folded motionless in her lap. "Why has the policeman been here? Twice now. What is he after?"

"Your guess is as good as mine."

"No," Grace Cathcart said. "Because you know the reason and I don't. And I want to know. What, for example, happened in Mexico City?"

Cathcart now wore a faint smile. "If you mean, did I ask the Enright woman to dinner with the idea of getting her into bed afterward, the answer is yes, I did. I have an idea she would be quite something in bed."

"Unlike me?"

"Too many times, yes."

"Have I ever refused you?"

"Not overtly. But sometimes you might as well have. Since you ask."

Nothing had changed in Grace Cathcart's face. She said, "I still want to know what the policeman is after. He is not stupid, you know. Nor am I." She paused. "I am just purposely blind sometimes. There is a difference."

"I don't know what he is after."

Grace was silent, waiting, watching him steadily.

"All right," Cathcart said, "I *think* he thinks I had something to do with the Harrington boy's death."

"Did you? You were almost paranoid about him, and I have always wondered why."

"Because he was a damned nuisance."

"Did he tap your telephone?"

Cathcart studied her carefully. "Where did you hear that?"

"From the policeman. I don't know where he heard it."

Cathcart pushed back his chair and stood up. Angrily he switched off the computer and walked across the room and back. "He tapped my phone, yes. I couldn't prove it, but he did. Why, I don't know, but I didn't like it. I had him charged with vandalism, but the judge, that stupid *chicano* juvenile judge, threw the charge out."

"The policeman," Grace said, "wondered why you were so upset by the possibility of a phone tap. So do I, now that you tell me this. The charge came up in juvenile court? Then he must still have been just a boy."

"He was."

"What harm could a boy do you by listening to your phone conversations?"

"What harm he could do doesn't matter. It's the principle."

Grace smiled. "I don't believe you have principles. I don't recall seeing them."

"That's a cheap shot."

"Is it? You just admitted you tried to get the anthropologist into bed in Mexico. Nor was that the first time, the policeman said."

Cathcart had stopped his pacing. "No, it wasn't. And there have been others. But at least they were all women."

There was a change in Grace Cathcart's face then, subtle, but visible. But her voice remained cool, quiet. "And what does that mean?"

"You," Cathcart said, "and other women. At least I play it straight."

"I see." Grace Cathcart took her time. "Yes," she said at last, "I, and other women. I enjoy them. More than I enjoy you. Much more." She paused, still watching him. "Does that answer the question you were afraid to ask?" She waited, but there was no

165

reply. "So now that we have that matter straight," she said, "let's return to my original question. What is the policeman after? And why does he think you are involved?"

"I don't know."

For long moments Grace remained sitting quietly, her hands in her lap and her eyes fixed on his. She said at last, "I don't believe you." She stood up then. "But I don't intend to have him think that I am involved too," she said.

Cathcart's expression was wary now. "So what are you going to do?"

"I don't know. Yet." Grace turned away and walked out of the room.

Cathcart watched her slim back until it disappeared around the bend in the hallway. His expression was thoughtful, even somewhat menacing.

14

Cassie did not tell Johnny of the telephone call she had received. She did not see that there was anything he could do about it, and she was sure it would anger him. Maybe later, she told herself, when some of the effect of the call had worn off and she could be dispassionate, even analytical, she would mention it, but not now.

Instead, after dinner that night she sat with Johnny on the sofa, looking into the piñon fire while he told her about his two interviews that day. Chico lay at their feet, rolling his eyes from one to the other as they spoke.

"Penny Lincoln," Johnny said, and shook his head. "Crazy, mixed-up kid—that phrase is almost worn out from too much use, but it applies here. She knows she can't paint. She knows she's not good at much of anything. Sam had it right; the girl's only got one thing to sell."

Cassie said slowly, "You think Charley Harrington used her?"

Johnny turned to look at her. "Explain that, *chica.*"

"You think that from Grace Cathcart, Penny got information about Ross Cathcart? Maybe without even knowing it? Just absorbing it from Grace's idle, relaxed talk?"

"You see it that way too?" Johnny nodded, pleased. "Flora Hobbs thought it might be possible."

"And then she, Penny, passed it along to Charley Harrington—again without realizing that she was saying anything important? That's how you see it?"

"He made her feel like what she said was important," Johnny said. "That's what she told me. Only she didn't see the implications."

Cassie said slowly, "How much does Grace Cathcart know about Ross's business—or other activities? Are they close? I don't pretend to understand either one of them."

"Tampoco, neither do I." Johnny was silent for a few moments, staring again at the flames as if answers glowed there. "They both seem so damned— polished, to a high gloss, I mean, so shiny that everything is reflected instead of being absorbed. How could either one of them be close to anybody?" He turned his head then to look at Cassie.

"Ross Cathcart," Cassie said, "is not impenetrable. I saw him when he was frightened, and trying hard not to show it, but not succeeding."

"And," Johnny said, "like I told Mark Hawley, I don't see anything in pork bellies or winter-wheat futures to cause that. Or to bring in the kind of bad *hombres* you described."

"You think—dope?" Cassie said, and, answering her own question, nodded. "I had the same feeling, and I couldn't say why. But how? We read about it, but how does it actually get here? And why here?"

"On its way to California," Johnny said. "And they're called mules—the ones who bring it in, usually by car, through Juarez, El Paso, and on up through New Mexico." He made a quick gesture of dismissal. "That's Fed business, Treasury; Bureau of Alcohol, Narcotics, and Firearms, I think it's called, or Drug Enforcement Agency. What Mark Hawley wants me to stay out of."

"How or where could Ross Cathcart fit in?"

Johnny showed his quick smile. "Good question, *chica*. Obvious too. Only I just hadn't gotten around to asking it yet." He was silent, staring again at the flames.

"He is a money man," Cassie said. "Commodities, stocks, trading—"

"Keep going," Johnny said. "That leads where?" He was thinking of Lucille and Waldo's idea of a Swiss bank account. "He would know how money moves, which I don't."

"I've never had enough of it to worry about," Cassie said, "but wouldn't what we're talking about have to be in cash? At first, I mean? Checks leave a trail. Bills are—anonymous."

Again half-hidden thoughts like mice in the shadows scurried around the edges of Johnny's mind and were gone, leaving behind only a feeling of close proximity. Johnny stood up and stretched. "Too many questions," he said, "too few answers. *Basta!* Enough!" He smiled down at Cassie. "A quick stroll outside for the three of us, and then bed, *chica?*"

Cassie's smile was brilliant. "I accept with pleasure."

Monica Jaramillo closed the Johnson Gallery as usual that night, and, as she sometimes did, stopped by Sam's for a drink on the way home. She sat at the bar, and presently Sam came along behind the bar to chat. Monica greeted her with a smile. "How're things?" Sam said. "Busy at the gallery?"

Still smiling, "This is the slow season. Things will pick up when the skiing starts and the Californians come to town with their checkbooks. It used to be the Texans." Monica paused. "Same with you, no?"

"I'm a little luckier," Sam said. "Folks have thirsts all year round, but trade does pick up when the ski lifts open." Sam liked Monica—admired her poise, was attracted by her looks, and recognized kindred appetites in her. One day, Sam had often thought, she and Monica Jaramillo might well decide to . . . get together. It was pleasant to think about sometimes.

Monica said, "You know that police lieutenant pretty well, don't you? That Johnny Ortiz?"

"We get along." Sam smiled. "No community of interests, but I like him. He is *mucho hombre,* much man."

"As Roberto Lewis found out, yes." Monica's smooth face was contemplative. "The hard way," she added.

"I never knew much about that," Sam said. "I knew you and Roberto were—" She hesitated, searching for a polite way to put it.

"Shacked up together," Monica said easily. "Yes. Things were a little tough for me then, and it was . . . convenient." She shrugged her slim shoulders. "When it . . . blew up, Ross Cathcart came up with a job offer at the gallery, so it all worked out."

"The papers," Sam said, "were never quite clear what happened."

Monica shrugged again. "Roberto had a temper. He let it get away from him one night. I wasn't there. The charge was murder two."

Sam rubbed a nonexistent spot from the polished bar. "I remember now," she said. "He worked for Ross Cathcart then, didn't he?"

"He ran errands for him down into Mexico. Roberto speaks good Spanish. I guess maybe Cathcart felt some kind of obligation, so I got the job offer."

Sam found another nonexistent spot and concentrated on wiping it away. "You asked about Johnny Ortiz," she said without looking up. "Anything in particular?"

"Just that he came into the gallery. And I've been wondering why. I wouldn't have thought of him as interested in art."

"No," Sam said, "neither would I." She was studying Monica's face now and what she saw there piqued her interest. "Another drink?" She smiled. "On the house. Things are slow, and it's nice to have somebody to talk to." She took the empty glass from the bar. "The same?" And busied herself with bottle and jigger. "Johnny," she said as she set the fresh drink in front of Monica, "usually doesn't go places or do things without a reason, you know what I mean?"

"I do," Monica said. "That's what bothers me. He's

171

so damned—Indian sometimes." Her smile was a trifle unsteady. "It gives me the creeps."

"His scalping-knife look," Sam said, and nodded. "I know just what you mean." For whatever reason, Sam thought, there seemed to be a far closer rapport between Monica and herself this evening than there had ever been—maybe even the beginning of what might become closeness. Perhaps this was the time she had often thought about? "You're worried about something?" she said. "Because of Johnny, I mean?"

Monica was silent for a little time, staring down at her drink. She raised her eyes to meet Sam's again. "I'm not sure," she said. "I just don't know."

"Would talking help?"

Monica smiled faintly and lifted her shoulders in an uncertain shrug.

"I don't mean here," Sam said. "Too many ears. Like I said, business is slow tonight. Bessie can take over. Shall we go to my place where we can be private?"

There was no hesitation. "I think I would like that," Monica said.

Johnny went to Joseph Whitney's law office the next morning, by appointment, already convinced that coming straight to the point would be the best approach. "I knew you were Charley Harrington's lawyer, of course," he said, "but I didn't know until yesterday that you also represent Ross Cathcart."

Whitney smiled faintly, wholly at ease. "I have a number of clients, Lieutenant. I hardly saw any necessity for naming them all."

"Understood. But when you came to me with a

hint, more than a hint, that Cathcart and Charley Harrington had had unusual money dealings—"

"About which, Lieutenant," Whitney said, "you will remember I made it quite plain that I wanted no definite knowledge. I came to you then, as I told you at the time, because as an attorney, an officer of the court, I felt it was my obligation to bring my suspicions to light."

"No conflict of interest, Counselor, in pointing a finger at a client? At two clients, as a matter of fact?"

"A matter of conscience. And I am comfortable with my decision. In those matters in which I represented Charley and continue to represent Ross, I have always been meticulous in my behavior, giving each the best advice and legal service that is in my power. I am completely comfortable with that too."

"Night before last," Johnny said, "you met Ross Cathcart at the airport in Albuquerque?"

Whitney shook his head at the implication. "Our meeting was quite by chance, Lieutenant. I was there to meet another friend who had also flown up from Texas. I had no inkling that Ross was on the plane."

"Who was the other friend?"

"Does it matter, Lieutenant?"

Johnny shook his head. "I don't know."

Whitney was smiling now. "But it is certainly no secret. His name was, is Inocencio Valdez. He lives in El Paso but travels extensively. He had boarded the aircraft at San Antonio. He drove back to El Paso yesterday. Does that satisfy your curiosity?"

Johnny stood up. "Thanks for your time, Counselor."

"Any time. I am always happy to cooperate with the

authorities." Whitney raised a hand suddenly. "A moment, please. You might like to know that both Lucille and Waldo Harrington have accepted their appointments to the board of the Charles Harrington Foundation. They insisted on waiving all remuneration, which I thought was quite generous of them." Whitney produced his smile again. "Of course, as beneficiaries of Charley's life insurance policy—" He shrugged. "One million dollars is quite a bit of money."

"So I have always understood," Johnny said. *"Hasta luego, señor abogado."*

"Hasta luego, señor teniente."

Whitney's Spanish accent, Johnny noted, was flawless.

Lucille Harrington came to see Johnny that morning, and again as she sat quietly, her hands resting in her lap, he admired her poise and extraordinary *presence,* a blend of physical attractiveness and obvious mental capabilities. She employed no wiles, but the total effect nonetheless was intensely feminine and even vaguely erotic. Much woman, he thought in Tony Lopez's phrase.

"I have a rather odd question," Lucille said, and smiled. "Would it annoy you if Waldo and I arranged to have Ross Cathcart's telephone *swept*—I believe is the word—to see if it is indeed tapped?"

"He has three telephones," Johnny said, "and a computer."

Lucille thought about it for only a moment. "I see no problem in sweeping them all, if you have no objections?"

"None at all." Johnny showed white teeth in a quick

grin. "I won't even know about it." He hesitated. "Unless Cathcart protests, that is."

"I don't believe he will." Lucille studied Johnny's face. "You would probably prefer," she said, "not to know how we intend to go about it?"

Again the quick grin. "I'm sure I wouldn't understand if you told me," Johnny said.

Lucille stood up and extended her hand. Its grip was strong, friendly. "Thank you," she said. "You are a pleasure to work with."

Johnny watched her walk down the hallway. Heads turned as she passed. A woman who would make her presence felt in any company, he thought, and found himself wondering just how she and Waldo *were* going to go about their project. Probably with unusual methods, he decided. One day he would like to hear about it.

Lucille drove home where Waldo and a man named Peterson were waiting. "No problem," Lucille told them. "Johnny is far more perceptive *and* cooperative than many if not most members of the congressional committees I have to deal with."

Waldo nodded and turned to Peterson. "It's all yours, Pete. Care to tell us how you'll go about it?"

"Duck soup," Peterson said. "A pal of mine in the phone company will set it up to establish my bona fides. I'll take it from there. You don't care about the gory details." He smiled. "Not that you wouldn't understand them."

In his youth Peterson had worked for the telephone company and later, with a Ph.D. following his name, had worked as a scientist at the Bell Laboratories. He was now, and for some years had been, a senior physicist at the Scientific Lab specializing in electronics research and development. On occasion his expertise had been requested and gratefully used by various government agencies and bureaus in Washington. "By inclination and trade I'm a tinkerer," he liked to say.

As he walked to the door now, "Shouldn't take more than a couple of hours," he told Waldo and Lucille. "I'll get back to you soonest."

Lucille and Waldo walked back into the house. "Did it ever occur to you," Lucille said, "to wonder why Charley had this apparent antipathy for Ross Cathcart?"

"It has," Waldo said, "and I have found no answer."

"Or maybe," Lucille said thoughtfully, "we are making the mistake of thinking there had to be a reason beyond mere avarice." She paused. "I hope that wasn't all it was."

It was a question Johnny had not yet asked himself.

But Johnny did have another question on his mind this morning, and he waited until Tony Lopez came back from a coffee break to ask it. "Inocencio Valdez," he said. "Mean anything to you?"

Tony thought about it and shook his head. "I know a dozen Valdezes, but no Inocencio." He even permitted himself a small joke, a play on the Spanish name. "One or two that I know are not what you might call innocent, either."

Johnny nodded. "I'm wondering about this one." He reached for the phone.

Mark Hawley was in his office and immediately interested. "I'll have the name checked. He lives in El Paso, you say?"

"And is an old friend of Joe Whitney's," Johnny

added. "Whitney, by the way, is Cathcart's lawyer as well as Charley Harrington's. Does that mean anything to you?"

"Negative, son. Should it?"

"I don't know." There was entirely too much he did not know, Johnny told himself, and decided it was about time he tried to put things together and see if they added up to anything recognizable. "I'll be in touch," he said into the phone, hung up, and pushed back his chair. To Tony, he said, "I'll be out and around. If anything turns up—"

"I will see that you are found."

It was good to be out in the cool, fall air again and free of the confining walls. The great mountains looked down, their slopes showing the brilliant autumn gold of aspens against the evergreen forest; in the clear, high air a sight for how many artists to drool over? How many times had he, Johnny, read of the "clarity of the light" here in the Santo Cristo area, something he had never really noticed himself, but had simply taken for granted?

Walking at his usual, relaxed pace, which was faster than it seemed, he let his mind wander where it would, trying not to focus it, but, rather, letting it remain open and receptive to whatever ideas might bubble up out of its subconscious.

Taken for granted—the phrase repeated itself like a jingle that would not go away. Taken *what* for granted? He looked up again at the golden masses of aspen. Taken for granted that Charley Harrington—what? Knew too much? About whom? Cathcart? Likely, even almost certain, if, as Johnny suspected, Cathcart's telephone line had been tapped. Bless Lucille and Waldo for arranging to find out for sure.

But why had Charley Harrington gone to the trouble to tap the line in the first place? A brilliant kid, feeling his oats and wanting to demonstrate how brilliant he was? It didn't fit. Charley Harrington already knew beyond any doubt what his capabilities were, and, given what Johnny knew of the boy, would not have given a damn about proving himself to anybody.

Okay, start with that presumed tap. What did Charley want to know about Cathcart that would motivate him in that direction? Money? That would be an obvious motive, somehow to turn knowledge of Cathcart's affairs into cash that he, Charley Harrington, could, as Joe Whitney had said, use to build up his infant CH Company?

It didn't fit, no matter what Joe Whitney had said, because Charley was apparently able almost at will to tap the resources of the bank via their computer system, use the money, and then, when they finally caught up with him, pay it back with interest, his needs satisfied and his current goal accomplished. And obviously the bank would have more money than Cathcart so why even bother with the telephone tap?

No. *If* the tap were real, then there had to have been another motive for making it—and again those half-seen thoughts scurried on mice feet around the edges of his consciousness, and were gone.

Johnny did begin to focus his mind now, concentrating on Cathcart. Could he visualize the man, he asked himself, shotgun in hand, blasting Charley Harrington? The answer was no, not on the evidence of Cassie's assessment of Cathcart's fright in Mexico City and on the plane, and on his own assessment of the man.

Cathcart was a man of intellect, not action; pork-belly futures, stocks and bonds, fishing and play-going and collecting art occupied his life, and a scattergun loaded with double-ought buckshot just did not figure.

But Cathcart might have arranged it; that Johnny might be able to accept if evidence were to appear. Cathcart's associations—witness the Mexico City episode—would seem to be suspect. And, as Johnny had explained to Mark Hawley, only one conclusion concerning Cathcart and his activities seemed to fit all the facts—dope.

There *was* dope, a great deal of it, coming through New Mexico on its way to the big centers in California. That was a given. And dope, currently cocaine in particular, was highly lucrative. Assume that Cathcart was in the business, what then? What would be his role? Certainly he would not be one of the mules who carried out the actual transportation. Cathcart was—Johnny kept going back to it—a man of intellect, not of action, so his role would be white collar as opposed to a blue collar one in which he would actually get his hands dirty.

A money man, presumably wise in the ways of finance. Would large sums pass through his hands? Almost certainly. And if that were indeed the fact, then—*"Estúpido!"* he said under his breath, directing the term straight at himself. *"Cretino!"* Of course, of course. . . .

He looked around to check his location and then headed straight back for his office. He was smiling.

Lucille Harrington was back in Johnny's office that early afternoon. "There *is* a telephone tap," she said. "It is ingenious, we are told by an expert, unlike any other tap he has ever encountered." Was there a touch of pride in that statement? Apparently Lucille thought there was, because she smiled quickly in self-deprecation. "I realize that I am speaking of my son." The smile spread. "At least I assume that Charley was the originator of the tap."

"I think we can accept that as fact," Johnny said. And he thought he now knew the reason for it, but there was no need to make it plain yet. "Did your expert remove the tap?"

"No." Lucille hesitated. "He dissembled with Ross Cathcart." The smile now was almost conspiratorial. "Mr. Cathcart may have the impression, as a matter of fact, that the tap *has* been removed."

"Good," Johnny said, and added, "What you're telling me is strictly unofficial." He too was smiling.

"I appreciate that," Lucille said. "It is my preference too."

"Three telephones—" Johnny began.

"All are tapped. As is the computer. The method used is, as I said, most ingenious. And highly technical. But if you—"

Johnny raised one hand, palm out in refusal. "Explanation would be over my head." He was silent for a little time, thinking hard. "But, if, unofficially, I wanted to use the tap—" he began.

"Either Waldo or I could explain the procedure," Lucille said. Her tone altered, took on a new firmness. "I believe it fair to say that either of us is prepared to do whatever is within our capabilities to further your investigations." She paused briefly. "I intend to find out who killed my son, and, if possible, why." She paused again. "And," she said, "I assure you that any information that passes between us will be treated with strict confidentiality."

"Agreed." Again Johnny was silent for a little time, deep in thought. "You may not know," he said at last, "that others are quite interested in Ross Cathcart too. Or maybe you do know that already?"

"I had the impression that Congressman Hawley had an interest, yes. He did not tell us, and we did not ask, why."

"He's a wily old bird," Johnny said, "and he holds his cards close to his vest. He has warned me off Cathcart."

Lucille's calm eyes studied Johnny carefully. "I see. But you are not obeying the warning." She nodded. "I can appreciate your position. And ours." She hesitated only a brief moment, and Johnny had the impression that her mind was functioning at computer speed. "It would seem," Lucille said then, "that we have what might be considered a bargaining chip, don't you think?"

"Knowledge of the tap," Johnny said nodding, "and the technical expertise to exploit it, yes." It pleased him that she had recognized the fact. His admiration for her continued to grow.

"Mr. Cathcart," Lucille said, "may be a despicable man, but my only interest in him, and Waldo's only interest as well, concerns his relationship to Charley. Whatever else he may or may not do means nothing to us."

"I can't quite say the same," Johnny said, thinking now of Cassie and her experience in Mexico City, "but up to a point we do look at Cathcart the same way."

"Allies," Lucille said. She was smiling.

"Definitely." Johnny pushed back his chair and stood up. "What do you say to our going together to talk to Mark Hawley?"

Lucille rose from her chair too. She was still smiling. "I was about to suggest it."

Outside again in the clear, cool, fall air they walked in step toward the Federal Building. Lucille said, "The aspens are turning brilliantly. You have noticed?"

"With pleasure." Simple truth.

"A friend of ours, an artist," Lucille said, "commented the other day that in New York he had always found fall a sad season, but that he doesn't have the same feeling at all here, and he thought he had finally figured out why. It is because in the East, fall means a farewell to the sun until spring. Not so here."

Johnny had never thought of it in that way, and said so. "I don't think I could handle that," he added. "The sun—" He stopped, and his sudden smile turned inward, mocking his thoughts. "—and the mountains and the space all mean too much to me." The smile spread. "That's the Indian part of me speaking." It suddenly occurred to him that before Cassie he would never, never have been able to say something like that, or even think it without bitterness and pain. Now, with this woman, it was merely easy, comfortable conversation. Little reminders like this, he thought, kept turning up to show him how precious to him Cassie was.

"Such beautiful country," Lucille said, "and yet there are the . . . ugly things that happen. They shouldn't. To me they are almost sacrilege, and I am not religious."

Mark Hawley was in, and he closed the inside office door after them. He waited until Lucille was seated before he sat down behind his desk and studied them both. "A conference," he said, and nodded. "Friendly? Or otherwise?"

"We come in peace," Johnny said, and, unbidden, an almost forgotten word came to mind: "A *palaver.*" He noted the small smile that appeared on Lucille's lips.

The congressman looked from one to the other in question.

"Johnny speaks for us both," Lucille said.

"Well, now," the congressman said, his face suddenly expressionless, "it seems you have the floor, son. Speak your piece."

Johnny nodded. "We have information we think you could find very useful."

Mark Hawley wore his poker face now. "In exchange for what?"

"Cooperation."

"Big word, son. It means just about whatever you want it to mean. Care to give me a hint?"

"You be the judge. Cathcart's telephones, all three of them, *and* his computer, are tapped. That is confidential and unofficial, of course."

Hawley's face was a study in stone. "Showing your hole card right off the bat?" he said.

"No." This was Lucille Harrington. "This is not an ordinary tap, one easily found by a run-of-the-mill technician. Nor is it easily used once it is found. You may believe that, congressman."

The congressman thought about it. "I guess I'll have to," he said at last. "Electronic wizardry is out of my line. Of course I might bring in an expert of my own—"

"I doubt it," Lucille said, and there was finality in her tone. "We had the best."

Again the congressman hesitated. He stood up at last and walked around his desk to the wall cupboard from which he took a decanter and three glasses and set them on his desk. "Let's have a drink and talk about it. You, ma'am?"

"Thank you," Lucille said, again surprising Johnny.

"I'll go along," Johnny said, and accepted his glass.

Mark Hawley sat down again and raised his own drink. "Peace," he said, and sipped the whiskey. His eyes studied them both. "What kind of cooperation?"

he asked. "Let's lay it out where we can study it. Like the man said, all unofficial. And confidential."

Sam opened the bar on that day in a thoughtful mood. Far more than she had anticipated had come out of Monica Jaramillo's visit to her house last night, and an important part of it was definitely food for thought, even concern. Sam went about her routine chores in an almost absent-minded fashion which was totally unlike her.

Penny Lincoln came in earlier than usual, ordered her glass of white wine, and then, instead of retreating to her customary corner table, perched on a bar stool as if prepared to talk. Her opening gambit caught Sam's attention at once.

"That Indian cop," Penny said, "scares the hell out of me." She shivered and had a deep sip of wine. "Know what I mean?"

"Johnny," Sam said in an unconcerned voice, "scares a lot of people, but they're mostly folks who have something to be scared about."

"Well, I haven't!" The tone was unnaturally belligerent.

"You ought to know," Sam said, and moved along the bar to take care of another customer. When she came back, Penny was still there, apparently waiting. Her wine glass was empty, and she pushed it across the bar toward Sam.

Sam filled it in her usual neat, economical fashion, conscious that the girl continued to watch her with an odd intensity. "Something eating you?" Sam said as she put the filled glass down.

Penny looked both ways along the bar. No one was close. "He said," she told Sam in a low voice, "that

Charley may have been killed because he knew too much."

Sam used her trick of polishing an invisible spot on the bar top to keep her eyes averted while she listened. "Happens," she said. "All kinds get into trouble by knowing too much." It was closer to home than she liked, but she allowed no worry to show when she looked at the girl again.

"He said," Penny went on, "that maybe I know too much too." Again she shivered and drank deep.

Sam thought about it. "Do you?" she said at last, her voice still unconcerned.

"No!" It was almost a cry. And then, in a quieter but still intensive tone, "I mean, if I do, I don't know it! That's what gets me!" Her hand holding the stem of the glass was trembling. The wine sloshed about and a little spilled on the bar. Penny did not notice. "And if I don't know it, then how do I know what he's talking about?"

"Did you ask him?"

Penny shook her head. She was, Sam decided, very close to tears. "He asks the questions. I mean, you don't feel like you'd better ask anything yourself!"

True enough, Sam thought; even if you did ask Johnny a question, like as not you'd get an ambiguous answer, or none at all. Johnny listened better than he talked, and, she remembered vividly, while he listened, he looked at you with those dark, somehow-angry eyes, and you couldn't even begin to tell what he was thinking. "Well," she said, "you knew Charley Harrington about as well as anybody, didn't you?"

"I . . . guess so." Penny's eyes seemed to cling to Sam's, imploring her for sympathy and understanding. "He didn't have many—friends," Penny added, and then shook her head. "I wasn't really a—friend. You know what I mean?"

"Why, I have a fair idea," Sam said.

"So why would I know anything? I mean, about what?"

"Beats me," Sam said, and moved along the bar again to a man who had just finished his beer and looked as if he wanted another. When she returned, Penny was still there, and her glass was empty again. "You're tossing them down pretty fast," Sam said. "Better watch it. It's early yet."

"I can pay," Penny said, "if that's what you're thinking." She put a twenty-dollar bill on the bar. "See?"

"Put it away," Sam said. "I'm not worried about that." She wondered idly if the money had come from Grace Cathcart. Likely, she thought. She was surprised to hear herself saying suddenly, "Look, Penny, what are you doing here, anyway? In Santo Cristo, I mean?"

"I'm an artist." The girl's lower lip was trembling. "Okay, maybe I'm not really. But I like the . . . people. Or, I did. Now—" She caught the lower lip between her teeth and blinked hard, trying to control herself.

"You have it bad," Sam said. What the girl needed, she thought, was somebody to put her over their knee and paddle some sense into that vacuously pretty head. "You don't belong here," she said. "In Santo Cristo either you earn your way, or you earn it someplace else and then come here to enjoy it. You don't fit either way." She was losing her goddamn mind, she thought angrily, letting herself do what she never did—give advice. Taking care of Sam, she always said, was a fulltime business and the only one that concerned her. Then why this?

"Where would I go?" Penny said. It was almost a wail.

"Damn it," Sam said, "how would I know? I don't even know where you're from!" With the forlorn ones like Penny, you never did know. They just turned up like stray kittens or superannuated babies left on strange doorsteps, unable to believe they wouldn't find somebody who would love them and take care of them. "Maybe you'd better get drunk, at that," Sam said, and moved along the bar.

When she returned, Penny had taken her wine to the corner table and was sitting there alone. She looked somehow smaller, Sam thought, as if she had been caught in the rain and had shrunk.

Concentrate on your own worries, Sam told herself; Penny and all the others like her are no business of yours.

Cassie had a visitor too that day: Grace Cathcart, slim and stunning in her tailored frontier trousers, polished boots, and beige silk shirt. Not a hair of her sleek coiffure was out of place. "I hope I am not intruding," Grace Cathcart said. "I have a favor to ask."

"Sit down," Cassie said, and smiled.

"You are lovely when you smile," Grace said. "It brings out a kind of . . . inner beauty." She seated herself, gracefully, as she did all things.

Chico's head appeared. He looked at the visitor,

who held out a hand which he sniffed politely, and then withdrew to his place beneath the desk.

"The lieutenant," Grace Cathcart said. "Your friend, John Ortiz I believe is his name."

"What about him?"

"He seems perpetually angry."

Cassie smiled again and said nothing.

For long moments Grace Cathcart studied Cassie's face and then nodded. "I see you would rather not talk about him." She hesitated. "But I am only interested in what he thinks."

"About what?"

"About me."

"I'm afraid," Cassie said, "that you'll have to ask him that. I don't think I really know."

"About my husband then."

"Pretty much the same answer," Cassie said. "I'm sorry, but Johnny likes to say what he thinks himself."

"He doesn't say very much very often."

"It's the way he is." Cassie was still smiling.

"He said," Grace Cathcart said slowly, carefully, "that in Mexico City my husband invited you to dinner. With the hope of getting you into bed afterward."

"He asked me to dinner, yes," Cassie said. "I could only guess at what he had in mind."

"He admits his motive."

"Then you have the answer, don't you?"

There was not so much as a hint of a frown on Grace's face, but her eyes had changed. They now seemed more intense. "I have no idea what your lieutenant suspects my husband of doing," she said. "But I would like him to know that whatever it is, I have no part in it. As I explained, I know nothing of my husband's business activities. He says himself that my only interest in them is in the money they produce, and, to a point, that is true."

"I'll be happy to pass that word to Johnny." Cassie's voice was quiet, matter-of-fact. "Whether he will take it at face value or not, I have no idea."

"Do you enjoy the theater?" Grace Cathcart said, abruptly changing the subject.

"I haven't seen many plays. Tickets are expensive."

"It is *Doctor* Enright, isn't it?"

"A Ph.D.," Cassie said, "not a medical degree. And I rarely use the title."

Again Grace Cathcart was silent for a little time. Her eyes did not leave Cassie's. She said at last, "I sense a certain . . . antipathy in you. Is it directed toward me?"

Cassie too took her time. "As an anthropologist," she said, "I am accustomed to dealing with so-called primitive peoples. You certainly do not fall into that category."

Grace Cathcart stood up. Her expression had not changed, and there was no annoyance in her voice. Only her eyes betrayed resentment. "I think," she said, "that you are not nearly as naive and uncertain as you like to appear, Dr. Enright. A pity. I think we might have been friends."

Cassie's smile reappeared. "As I said, we are not quite on the same plane, so I'm afraid I doubt it."

"Thank you for your time." Grace Cathcart walked down the hallway, tall, erect, slimly rounded, impeccable in appearance. Cassie watched her until she disappeared down the stairs.

* * *

"And that was how it went," Cassie said that night after dinner, sitting in front of the piñon fire. She waited quietly for Johnny's reaction.

"She swung and she missed," Johnny said, and nodded. "But it was a good try."

"What was she trying to accomplish? That's what puzzles me."

Johnny produced one of his rare smiles. "Plain enough, *chica*. She doesn't want to talk to me. She doesn't like me, and she knows I don't have a very high opinion of her. So she does the next best thing, talks to you"—the smile even spread a little, softened —"because as *todo el mundo,* all the world knows, you are closer to me than anyone else."

"She was trying to dissociate herself from Ross Cathcart, her husband."

"Exactly. My guess is that she knows more about him than she would like to admit, and she wants to be no part of—whatever might happen to him."

"That means," Cassie said, "that she knows, or is reasonably sure, that he is doing something"—she turned to look at Johnny—"well out of line?"

"Probably. And she doesn't want to be an accessory. Smart woman."

Cassie shivered. "She gives me fits. She kept looking at me as I suppose she looks at that girl Penny Lincoln you told me about."

"You are well worth looking at, *chica*. Even by another woman."

Johnny went by the Fine Arts Museum on his way to his office the next morning. Even to his eye, which he considered untutored, there was no mistaking Sid Thomas's paintings, nor their quality. Completely representational, they stood out because of their realism that caught your breath and tempted you to reach out and touch.

He stayed looking at the paintings for a long time, absorbing their quiet, calm beauty, and remembering what Sid had told him about Charley Harrington's questions: How was it possible to show convincingly an enormous 12,400-foot mountain in all its majesty on a piece of canvas no more than two feet by three? Why did Sid exaggerate that corner of the building, and how could it be that, so exaggerated, it looked more real than real? How? Why? How? Probing questions from anyone, Johnny thought, let alone a boy—merely another measure of the boy himself.

He went up close to a few of the paintings and read the small plaques beneath. Each was marked: Museum Collection, Anonymous Donor. As Will Carston had said.

He walked on to his office in a thoughtful mood. Bit by tiny bit, he thought, the outlines of the jigsaw puzzle were beginning to appear in his mind. Now came the hard part: filling in the interior shapes and colors until the picture was whole.

"A visitor waiting," Tony Lopez said. "You are a very popular fellow."

Sam was sitting in Johnny's office, looking uncomfortable. "If you'd been five minutes later," she said as Johnny walked in, "I'd have been gone. I psyched myself up for this, and my resolve was oozing away."

There were times, Johnny thought, when Sam's speech, her use of words, indicated a well-educated background. Not for the first time he found himself wondering fleetingly where she had come from, and why. No matter; he doubted if he would ever find out. Many folks came here to Santo Cristo out of nowhere. He sat down and smiled faintly across the desk. "What—?"

"When you smile like that," Sam said, "you make a person think of ant hills—being staked out on one, I mean. If that's your welcoming expression, change it. Give me your scalping-knife glare. At least then I know where I stand."

Johnny's smile spread. "Bad night, Sam? You're jumpy this morning."

"With good reason." Sam sat quiet for a time,

scowling at the floor. She looked up at last. "I'm losing my marbles," she said. "I'm responsible for nobody but me. That's the way it is, and that's the way I like it. And here I am worrying about somebody who wouldn't even be worth worrying about for a professional do-gooder."

"Who would that be?"

"Penny Lincoln."

Johnny's smile disappeared. He leaned back in his chair now and stared briefly at the far wall. He looked at Sam again. "What's happened to her?"

"Nothing, yet, as far as I know. But the fool kid is scared spitless." Sam leveled a large forefinger at Johnny. "You put the fear of the Lord in her. Why? Trying to scare something out of the underbrush? Is she the tethered goat to attract the tiger? If so, why don't you pick on somebody your own size?"

"Maybe you'd better tell me the whole story," Johnny said, and sat quietly while Sam went through yesterday's bar encounter with Penny.

"When I closed up last night," Sam finished, "she was still sitting at that table, about as drunk as a girl could be and still manage to stay in a chair."

Johnny said gently, "What did you do?"

"Oh, hell," Sam said, clearly embarrassed, "I took her to her studio. Up on Canyon Road. It's—"

"I've seen it."

"Okay. Then you know what it looks like. I undressed her and put her to bed and even thought about cleaning up the mess a bit, but—"

"What mess?"

Sam looked surprised. "You said you'd seen the place. It's like a pigsty—only pigs left to themselves are clean. Penny isn't. Everything scattered from hell to breakfast, clothes, cooking utensils—what there was of them—paints, brushes, canvases. . . ."

"It wasn't that way when I saw it," Johnny said. "It wasn't *House and Garden,* but it wasn't a mess, either. And I woke her up when I pounded on the door, so she hadn't had time to straighten things up." He paused. "So tell me more."

Sam shook her head. "There isn't any more. If that's not the way she always lives, then—oh, hell, you mean somebody tore the place apart?"

"It looks that way, doesn't it?"

"Why? Looking for something? What does Penny have that's worth that? Cheap costume jewelry, rummage-sale clothes, a few painting things, and what else? Nothing!"

"Does she have a phone?" Johnny said.

Sam shook her head. "I doubt it. She gets calls at my place, messages."

Johnny was already on his feet.

"Where you going?" Sam said. And then, "Oh, migod! You think maybe somebody came back?"

"I'm going to find out."

Sam was on her feet too. "Not alone, you aren't. I guess I feel kind of responsible. And don't laugh, goddamn it! I feel silly enough as it is!"

From the outside, number five in the compound looked just as it had when Johnny had seen it before, no signs of damage. He knocked, heard no response, and tried the door. It opened easily, and he could hear the sound then—a small whimpering such as a lost and frightened puppy might make. "Stay here," he told Sam and went inside.

Sam had been accurate in her description. The little house was a mess—clothes, dishes, cooking utensils, painting equipment, the pitifully few books, and bric-a-brac all lying about where they had obviously been thrown.

Penny herself, naked and huddled in the fetal position, whimpering softly, lay on the floor of the tiny bedroom. When Johnny bent and touched her bare shoulder gently, she curled tighter and stifled a scream. "Don't!" she whispered. "Please don't! No more!"

Johnny straightened. The lines of his face were very harsh. "You'd better come in, Sam," he said as he looked around at the wreckage of the bedroom—the mattress torn off and ripped open, dresser drawers pulled out and their contents emptied on the floor, a lamp smashed and a chair overturned. . . .

Sam said, "Oh, migod!" and bent over the girl, her voice suddenly gentle, soothing, saying, "It's all right, Penny, all right. It's all over. We're here. It's all right." She saw Johnny start for the doorway and she said quickly, "Where're you going?"

"The car. Radio. Stay with her."

To Tony Lopez on the radio, "Get Doc Means. And Saul Pentland. To Penny Lincoln's place. *Pronto!*" He hung up the microphone and went back into the house.

Sam said, "Let's move her. I'll get her covered up."

"No." Johnny's voice was cold. "Don't touch anything. Doc Means is on the way, and a state police lab man. We'll wait for them."

Standing there in the bedroom doorway, looking down at the naked, huddled girl, the brutally devastated room, feeling the cold anger in his mind like a heavy, painful weight, he could nonetheless also think on another level with almost complete dispassion, finding in this evidence of unbridled savagery yet another piece that fitted neatly within the puzzle's frame.

Sam looked up at him, opened her mouth to speak, and then, seeing what was in his face and eyes, decided that silence was the more prudent course. She patted Penny's bare shoulder again. "Just hang in there, baby," she said softly. "Help's on the way."

Johnny sat again in Mark Hawley's office that midmorning. "She isn't entirely coherent yet," he told the congressman, "but we do have some of the facts. There were two men, both Hispanic. One spoke fair English, and he kept asking two questions: 'What did Harrington tell you?' and 'What did Harrington leave with you?'"

The congressman thought about it, his face expressionless. He said at last, "Go on, son. You didn't come here just to tell me that."

"What it means," Johnny said, "is that I'm cutting myself into whatever coverage you're putting on Cathcart. The connection is too plain, and this happened in my jurisdiction."

"You have a point," the congressman said mildly, "and we did agree on cooperation. So what do you want?"

"The names of all foreign nationals who were on the flight that brought Cassie and Cathcart here from San Antonio."

"Not from Mexico City?"

Johnny shook his head. "San Antonio to here."

"You're playing a hunch?"

"I'm guessing," Johnny said, "but I think it adds up. That phone call Cassie made from San Antonio giving flight arrival time, and telling me not to be there—those two facts I think are the key. Someone overheard the call, was meant to overhear it, and passed along the arrival time. Somebody here, somebody who didn't want me to see him, or her, was waiting, not for Cassie or Cathcart, but for two other passengers on the same flight."

"The thugs who beat up the girl?"

"They don't fool around, those people," Johnny said. "Any link from Cathcart to Charley Harrington to Penny Lincoln is farfetched, but they worked the girl over anyway just to be sure. They don't care what they do or who they hurt doing it."

"And you don't like it," the congressman said. "I don't blame you. I don't like it myself. You'll get the names and passport numbers, if any. What do you think they're after?"

"Your guess is as good as mine."

The congressman, smiling, bore a good resemblance to a crocodile in the shallows. "Somehow, I don't quite believe that, son, but we'll let it lie for the moment. You have ideas about what they might do next? Whoever they are?"

Johnny stood up. His face was carved in stone. "I have ideas," he said. "We'll see what happens."

The telephone on the congressman's desk rang softly then, and Hawley picked it up, spoke his name, and gestured toward Johnny. "For you. Cassie, I think."

It was Cassie. "I just heard what happened to Penny Lincoln," she said. Her voice was not quite steady. "I want to tell you something that maybe I ought to have told you before. I——"

"You're at your office? I'll be there right away." Johnny hung up.

"Trouble, son?" the congressman said, but Johnny had already gone through the door.

Cassie was at her desk, Chico beside her chair looking worried. "Maybe it doesn't mean anything," Cassie said. "But maybe——" She shook her head. "I had a phone call. In Spanish. The morning after I got back . . . " She recounted the call almost word for word.

"Yes," Johnny said when she was done, "you should have told me, *chica*. But it's all right now. I'll use your phone."

Old Ben Hart out in his stone ranch house answered the call himself. He listened, and then his big voice almost filled the office. "Love to have her, son. She lights the place up like a big fire in the hearth. And don't you worry a mite. Nobody'll bother her here."

Johnny hung up. For the first time that morning he could smile, and mean it. Pure relief. "That we can be sure of, *chica*. Nobody will bother you there. Not with Ben around."

"Johnny——"

"Until we get this straightened out, *chica*," Johnny said. He was smiling no longer. "I want you safe. Understood?" He waited for no answer. "And you're going there right now. I have things to do."

Tony Lopez, summoned, stood large and solid in Cassie's small office and heard his instructions. "Go by the house," Johnny said, "to pick up the few things she needs. Then Ben Hart's place. You have a riot gun in the car? Use it, if you have to. Two *chicanos,* maybe Mexican, maybe not, but—" He stopped. "You have the picture. No sense in my going over all of it."

"Claro," Tony said. "There will be no problem, *amigo.* I will deliver her safe and sound to *el oso pardo."*

El oso pardo, Johnny thought, the grizzly bear; it was an apt name for old Ben. Anyone invading Ben's ranch with bad ideas would have his head handed to him on a platter. He felt better as he kissed Cassie briefly. "Take care of yourself, hear?"

Her voice lacked its usual confidence. "I promise."

Johnny's next stop was Charley Harrington's house high on the hills behind the city. It was sealed with a police notice which did not seem to have been tampered with. Johnny let himself in with a key and prowled swiftly through the entire house.

Nothing that he could see had been touched. So far, so good. But logic dictated that sooner or later, and probably sooner, the house would be searched as Penny Lincoln's house had been. The puzzle was becoming plainer and plainer now, he thought as he drove back to his office; vague ideas were beginning to fit into theories which in turn produced facts that could be anticipated. *Bueno.*

Sam was in his office again, and again impatient. "I didn't get a chance to tell you what else I had in mind," she said. "Penny—" She stopped and shook her head angrily. "I hope you catch the bastards who did that," she said. "And if you need help staking them out on an anthill, I'll be available."

"We'll take care of them," Johnny said, and there

was that in his eyes and in his words that sent small shivers up and down Sam's spine.

"Okay," she said. "Now—" She hesitated. "I dislike trotting my private life out in front of anyone," she said, "least of all the law, but—" Her face was set. "Penny wasn't the only one telling me her troubles. I know, I know, behind a bar you hear all kinds wanting to tell you how tough and unfair the world is. But this was different. This was Monica Jaramillo."

Nothing changed in Johnny's face, but his mind came to instant alert. He said as casually as he could, "What did she allow?"

"I don't think I've ever heard you talk Texas before," Sam said, "but, never mind. You came to the gallery, she told me."

"True."

"And you just walked around, looked at things, asked a few questions, nothing specific."

"Also true."

"But it made her jumpy," Sam said. "And she asked me and I told her you didn't usually do things without some reason." Sam watched Johnny and waited.

"Go on," Johnny said.

"Some day," Sam said, "I'll get you in a poker game and we'll see just how good you are. Right now I think you're bluffing. We'll find out." She was silent for a few moments. "Reason she was jumpy," Sam said, "is some statuary they have at the gallery." She paused and studied Johnny's face. "Ring a bell?"

"You have the floor. You came here wanting to tell me about it."

"You're good, *amigo,*" Sam said. "I'll give you that. Okay, she *said* you didn't know how they make some of the statuary. Way I get it, it isn't solid bronze like most pieces of cast sculpture you see. It's bronze powder in some kind of plastic, polymer, I think is the name. But it looks like the real thing."

Johnny nodded. "And that's what made her nervous. I kind of thought it might."

"She was shacked up with Roberto Lewis when you put him away," Sam said. "Monica's afraid you'll think she's—tarred with the same brush is the way they used to say it in novels. And she isn't. That's why she's jumpy."

Johnny took his time, turning the entire matter over in his mind, looking at it from all sides. "She asked you to talk to me?"

"Not in so many words. But I said I'd see what I could do." Sam shook her head vehemently. "That's twice in two days I've let myself get mixed up in somebody else's business."

"You're getting soft, Sam."

"Ain't it the truth? So? About her, Monica?"

"A very attractive woman."

"Hell's fire, I know that! Why—?" Sam stopped. "Okay. I asked for it."

"She only works here in the gallery?" Johnny said.

"That's how I understand it."

"I checked," Johnny said. "Artwork for the Johnson Gallery comes up from Mexico air freight. It goes through customs at Albuquerque, and is brought up here by truck. All open and above board."

"Monica arranges the displays. She has an eye for that kind of thing."

"She does a good job." Johnny paused. "If selling artwork at a gallery was illegal," he said, "a good share of the business folks in Santo Cristo would be in deep trouble." He shook his head. "They aren't."

Sam studied his face and found nothing. "I can tell her that?"

"Why, yes, if you think it will make her feel any better."

Sam stood up. She let her breath out in a big sigh. "Sometimes you're a nice guy, *amigo*. Did you know that?" She held out her hand. "Thanks."

"De nada," Johnny said as he shook her hand, "it was nothing."

In October in Santo Cristo, even with daylight savings time, nightfall comes early. It had been totally dark for not quite an hour that night when the car, with only parking lights showing, drove slowly uphill past the house that had been Charley Harrington's, stopped a few hundred yards beyond, and, turning, came back to park headed downhill.

The car's dome light, disconnected, did not betray the opening of the door, and the man who got out was almost invisible in the mountain darkness as he walked down the drive to the house.

When he reached it and was well-hidden from the road above he produced a small flashlight, which he played on the door lock. From his pocket he pulled out a small metal tool and inserted it into the lock—

A light over the door came on, and Johnny's voice

said coldly in Spanish, "That is good. Stay where you are, and turn slowly, hands extended. So."

The man turned. Johnny held a cocked lever-action 30-30 carbine waist-high, pointed at the man's stomach. "Open your jacket slowly," Johnny said, "both sides. Good. Take the gun out carefully and put it on the ground. Slowly. Now move over to the dirt, off the blacktop. So. Your name?"

The man spat. Instantly the 30-30 went off with a bang and dirt flew immediately beside the man's left foot. Johnny levered another cartridge into the carbine's chamber. "There are four more rounds in the weapon," he said. "That was merely a warning. The next shot will not miss, and you will not walk again on that foot, ever. Is that understood?"

The man stood silent, uncertainty beginning to show. Clearly he had not expected this reaction.

"Last night," Johnny said, slowly, distinctly, each word falling like a stone, "you brutalized a girl and ransacked her house. We do not like that here. You found nothing, but that is beside the point. You will be made to pay—if, that is, you are still alive when we are finished here."

"In the United States," the man said, but his voice lacked conviction, "you cannot behave like this."

Johnny smiled. "We are alone. There is your gun, proof that I had to defend myself." The smile was not pleasant to see. "Some of my ancestors," Johnny went on, "enjoyed roasting people they did not like over slow fires or staking them out naked on anthills and smearing them with honey. At times, such as now, I can appreciate their feelings."

He held the cocked carbine casually in his right

hand, forefinger on the trigger, last three fingers and thumb wrapped around the small of the stock, the barrel pointed at the man's stomach. "Four rounds in the weapon," he said again. "One for each foot. One for your *cojones*. The last round for your belly so you will die slowly in great pain." He was silent then, angry eyes steady on the man's face, while he waited in quiet relaxation with that bone-bred patience of his.

The night was still. Somewhere an owl hooted and a dog barked in reply. The sounds were distant. Johnny waited, motionless, and watched beads of sweat appear on the man's forehead. Still Johnny made no move.

The man's eyes fell away and dropped to look at the rifle. Its muzzle was unwavering. Slowly the man moistened his lips and a bead of sweat rolled unnoticed down the side of his nose. "A bargain—" he began.

"No bargain." There was finality in the tone, and the silence grew and stretched until it seemed to fill the surrounding darkness.

Again the man moistened his lips. His eyes had not left the rifle. He was sweating freely now, but made not the slightest move to wipe his face or eyes. As if hypnotized by the rifle's muzzle he said slowly, each word an effort, "What is it you want?"

"Information."

"About—what?"

"Todo, everything."

The big main house, a stone bulk looming against the night sky, was dark and silent, as was the bunkhouse fifty yards distant. In the corral a horse stomped one hoof and blew out his breath with a lip-whuffling sound. Distantly, a single coyote raised his voice in song, which quickly became a chorus as others joined in. Ranch dogs in their pen answered in kind and for a time the night was filled with sound. Then gradually, silence fell again.

There was no moon and in the blackness overhead stars seemed almost close enough to touch—Orion, Rigel and Betelgeuse, the Pleiades, Andromeda, Cassiopeia and Auriga, among other, lesser bodies, all clearly on display.

Within the main room of the big house, its brick floors showing here and there Indian rugs of price, its huge fireplace still warm from the evening fire, its trophy heads wall-mounted and its massive furniture hand-carved and solid, there were only ordinary house sounds as heavy wooden beams gave off occasional nocturnal protests, and somewhere an outside vent reacted to the gentle night breeze.

The intruder moved silently toward the staircase that led to the gallery off which the bedrooms opened. In his hand he held a sleek, modern, automatic pistol—a Baretta—and he kept his mouth open as he breathed without sound.

He reached the foot of the staircase and had one foot on the first tread when the room suddenly filled with light, and Ben Hart's voice coming from the direction of the fireplace said in border-accented Spanish, *"Basta!* Enough!" And, in English, "Just hold it right there, stranger. I've been waiting for you."

The man turned, the Baretta held cautiously

pointed slightly downward. He looked at the huge old man, and at the clumsy, old-fashioned, single-action .45 revolver he held loosely in one big fist.

"Stand aside, *abuelo,* grandfather," the intruder said in passable English, "and I will not hurt you. But if you interfere—" He gestured menacingly with the Baretta. It was a mistake.

The big revolver moved faster than the man would have thought possible. The room was suddenly filled with the roar of its blast, and the man stared down unbelievingly at what was left of the hand that had held the Baretta, blood beginning to gush from the remnants of two fingers. The scream he heard was his own.

"Go right ahead and bleed," Ben Hart said, his voice utterly devoid of sympathy. "Brick floors clean up good. Just don't bleed on one of my Indian rugs, hear?"

Upstairs a door burst open and Cassie leaned over the railing to gape down from the gallery in shocked silence.

"It's all right, honey," Ben said. "We've got our visitor. You might throw down a towel so he can wrap up that hand. Then we can have a little talk, him and me, and you can go back to bed and sleep sound. There won't be any more excitement tonight."

Mark Hawley, summoned from bed, walked into Johnny's office and looked at both Johnny and Ben Hart for a little time in silence before he spoke. To Johnny he said, "You brought yours in whole. I'll grant you that. But what did you threaten him with to scare him half to death?"

"No threats. Just the facts."

Hawley looked at Ben. "And you—"

"Man starts waving a gun at me," Ben said, "and in my own house at that—" He shook his head slowly. "I tend to get annoyed. Wouldn't you?"

The congressman sat down. He sighed. "I suppose it wouldn't do any good to say that times have changed?"

"Not a damn bit," Ben said. "Because they haven't. Guns are still guns, and folks who wave them around had better be prepared for reactions." He pushed his hat back with one forefinger, exposing the area of white forehead. "Hell's bells," he said, "you sound like somebody's morals society. I recollect when you—"

"All right," the congressman said, and looked at Johnny. "Colombian nationals," he said. "That—"

"Charged with aggravated assault, battery, illegal breaking and entering, illegal possession of firearms—" Johnny waved one hand gently. "I'll think up other charges if necessary."

The congressman took his time. "How much do you know, son?"

"Quite a bit, but not enough yet. My man talked but he didn't know much."

"The Feds want jurisdiction."

"The Feds can howl at the moon. This is my jurisdiction."

"Ben's ranch is—"

"The state police have turned it over to me. It's all tied together."

The congressman thought about it. "All starting with Charley Harrington's murder?"

"More or less."

"Cathcart's involved?"

"In a way."

"You're not very helpful, son."

"Way I see it," Ben Hart said, "he don't aim to be, and I don't blame him. Two men dead, blasted apart with a scattergun. One girl beaten damn near to death. And Cassie next on the list beyond a doubt—" Ben shook his head. "You get real sanctimonious sometimes. Maybe too much Washington has rubbed off on you, too many committee meetings, things like that."

The congressman sighed again. He said, "I'm a public servant and most times I try to behave like one." He sighed again. "Between us, it would have been better if you'd pulled the trigger, son, and if you"—he looked at Ben—"had done more than just wing your man. It—"

"No," Johnny said. "You'll want their testimony eventually, or the Feds will."

Mark Hawley thought about it. At last he nodded. "Maybe you're right," he said. "You have a habit of being." He paused. "When do we get the whole story?"

Johnny shook his head. "When I have it. There are things I still don't know. But I will."

The congressman nodded briefly and looked again at Ben Hart. "Cassie?" he said. "She's—?"

"She's fine. My foreman's sitting on the bottom step of the gallery stairs with a thirty-thirty on his lap."

The congressman stood up. He looked at his watch. "Near to daylight," he said. He looked again at Ben Hart. "It's been a busy night. How about a drink at my office?"

Ben heaved himself out of his chair. "That," he said, "is the first sensible thing you've said since you got here. Maybe there's hope, after all."

The congressman looked at Johnny. "You, son?"

"I'll pass," Johnny said. "I've got a lot of thinking still to do."

He sat on long after they had left, staring at the wall and considering the empty areas that remained inside the puzzle. As in following a game trail, it was sometimes necessary to backtrack to see if he might have missed a turning, and sometimes to circle when the trail seemed to disappear, patiently casting in wider and wider helical circles until at last spoor showed itself and the relentless pursuit could again begin.

He had been right when he'd told Cassie that perhaps her ill-advised trip to Mexico City had indeed produced results, and, as he had put it, flushed somebody out of the chamisa. He was in no doubt that the two men who had brutally beaten Penny Lincoln had come to Santo Cristo as a direct result of Cassie's visit, and perhaps Cathcart's as well.

Precisely what they were looking for—and hoped to be put on the trail of by Penny or Cassie—was clear enough. It was money. In quantity. But that, unfortunately, was all that his man had said that he knew, and, considering the state he was in by the time Johnny was finished, Johnny was convinced he was telling the truth.

Tony Lopez appeared, morning-fresh, and leaned against the wall. "It seems you have been busy, *amigo.*" He shook his head slowly. "And that one who went up against Señor Hart?" He showed the white teeth briefly. "I would as soon go up against a real grizzly bear armed with only a willow switch. It would be safer."

Johnny nodded absently, his mind skittering off in

other directions. He pushed back his chair and stood up. "The bank," he said. "I'll be with Bert Clancy."

He was not exactly sure what he was after, but the feeling was strong that at least some of the answers lay in this direction, perhaps unknowingly even in Bert Clancy's mind. Bert must have spent a good deal of time worrying about Charley Harrington's depredations, and maybe he had learned more than he might have thought.

"Sure, I spent a lot of time thinking about him," Bert admitted. "But I didn't come up with any brilliant ideas. He was always two, three jumps ahead . . ." He shook his head sadly. "And he was a good customer too, always kept a high balance—even if sometimes it was with our own money."

"And he used the money he got out of you in his CH Company?" Johnny said. "You're sure?"

Bert swiveled uncomfortably in his chair. "Well, hell, that's how we figured it. What else would he use it for? He didn't have what they call a high lifestyle. Or a dope habit he had to keep feeding. He—"

"Bueno," Johnny said, and switched the subject. "How did he make out with the IRS? Do you know?"

Bert looked even more uncomfortable. "Not officially. But, well, I know some of the IRS people, and—" He spread his hands. "They wouldn't admit it, but he—that is, they—oh, hell, they were just as far behind Charley Harrington as we sometimes were. Couple times they were about to lower the boom on him, but gave up the idea because they were afraid of reversal in tax court that would make them look pretty silly."

Johnny sat silent, thinking about Charley Harrington.

"The thing is," Bert said, "he wasn't *greedy*. You know what I mean? He could have worked hornswoggles that would have *made* us get real mean and serious, and the IRS too, but he never went that far. Twenty-five thousand here, maybe forty thousand there—but we always got it back, and so, well, holding company policy, they didn't want publicity, so—" He spread his hands again. "Hell of a situation, with me right in the middle. And, damn it, I *liked* Charley, warts and all."

Johnny walked out into the plaza from the bank in a thoughtful mood. There was a chill in the air and not many tourists under the portal of the Palace of the Governors or just walking aimlessly around. The day was brilliant and the asymmetrical towers of the cathedral showed sharp against the intense blue of the sky. As Johnny looked at them idly their bells began to ring. A flock of pigeons, startled, almost exploded into the air from their resting places nearby.

Johnny sat down on one of the benches. He could have told Bert where some of Charley's money—no, the money in Charley's *possession*—had gone, but there was no point in it. It wouldn't have made Bert feel any better, or worse.

Johnny had the feeling, unmistakable, that he had almost all of the pieces, but he just couldn't make them fit together. It happened like that sometimes; one missing ingredient, maybe something simple and even seemingly extraneous, was the key, and until it turned up, the entire puzzle lay in apparently unrelated sections that simply would not mesh.

Something nagged at him as he walked back to his office, thinking that, having been up all night, he would do well to go home for a shower and a shave and a change of clothes. He said as much to Tony, and was almost out the door when what had been nagging at him came unbidden to mind. He turned back.

"That fellow you knew ran sheep over near Pecos," he said, "the one who used double-ought buckshot for coyotes. What was his name?"

Tony opened his mouth and closed it again carefully. He shook his head. "Began with an *R*," he said. "Roybal? No. Renaldo? No." He popped his fingers with the sound of a whip crack. "Rael. Estéban Rael. Why?"

"Just curious," Johnny said. "It bothered me that he had no name, that's all."

Tony said, "Are you seeing visions again?"

Johnny could even smile. "Not this time, I'm afraid." He walked out to his truck.

He was in the shower, well-lathered-up, when, as if a coin had dropped in a slot, wheels turned in his mind, and the small fact he had been searching for popped into view. He was smiling as he rinsed and then toweled himself dry. It was not a pleasant smile.

18

Back in his office, Johnny's first telephone call was to the Cathcart house—which had, he noticed as he looked it up, only one listed telephone number. Obviously the other two lines were confidential. One more item to tuck away in his mind.

Grace Cathcart answered the phone, as Johnny had hoped she would. "I understood," he said, "that you wanted to talk to me."

"I—" Grace Cathcart began, and there she stopped, obviously thrown off-balance. There was only silence on the line. Perhaps Cathcart was within earshot?

"I had your message from Cassie Enright," Johnny said, "but I think it will be better if you amplify it. In person." He paused. "If you would rather not come here to police headquarters, we might meet someplace else. Perhaps up on the ski-basin road, at the aspen lookout? The color is remarkable this year."

There was no hesitation, and the woman's voice was pitched again in its usual, self-contained tone. "That will be fine," she said.

"In an hour?"

"That will fit nicely."

Johnny's second call was to Will Carston, and the man's polite, cultured voice brought instantly to mind the huge, sumptuous house, the secluded patios, and the carefully tended and manicured grounds.

"The pictures young Harrington purchased and donated to the museum?" Will Carston said. "Yes, of course. If the facts are germane to your investigation, I shall be happy to tell you whatever I know."

"Did Sid know all about them? That they were donated by Harrington, I mean?"

"As far as I am aware, no." Was there a gentle smile in the voice? "As a matter of fact, since you bring it up, I believe Sid is of the opinion that I may have been the donor. He is a proud man, but it is his belief that I am, in his phrase, 'bloated rich' through no effort of my own, and while he has consistently refused all offers of open financial assistance, on the one or two occasions when I have purchased one of his paintings for the museum, he has raised no objections. In his own quiet way, he is quite aware of the quality of his work, and having it hung where it can be seen by many people gives him much pleasure."

"He deserves it," Johnny said, "although I am no judge."

"On the contrary," Will Carston said in his courtly

way, "I believe you are quite capable of appreciating Sid's quality."

Johnny said, "One more question, maybe a funny one. Do you know how the paintings were bought?"

"Yes. The museum made each purchase. Young Harrington did not wish to appear anywhere in the transaction."

"He gave the money to the museum, setting his own price?"

"That is correct."

"And in what form did he turn over the money to the museum?"

There was slight hesitation. "It is odd that you should ask that," Will Carston said. "Or, perhaps, in view of your investigations, it is not. The money was always forthcoming in cash. The trustees questioned the practice, but in the end decided to accept it. Anonymous donors are frequently . . . eccentric, and it was assumed that this was Harrington's particular eccentricity, so we humored him in order to have the gifts."

Bingo. "Thanks very much, Will."

"Not at all. However I can be of help."

Johnny hung up and sat quiet for a time. When at last he reached again for the phone, his thoughts were in order, and almost, if not quite, complete. He called Ben Hart's big house, and asked for Cassie.

Her voice when she came on the line was quiet, subdued. "I hoped you would call. Last night—"

"That's all over, *chica*. Sorry, but that's the way it had to be."

"I was the bait?" Then, quickly, "Don't answer that. It was because I went down to Mexico City, no?"

"Yes."

"I've learned my lesson."

Johnny could smile then, and mean it. "Maybe yes, maybe no, *chica,* but it doesn't matter now."

"May I come home?"

"Not yet. I'm taking no chances. You're safe there—"

"A man named Fred is at the foot of the stairs with a rifle."

Johnny's smile spread. "So Ben said. That's good."

"Johnny, last night, that man—his hand!"

The smile disappeared. "Folks who wave guns around, *chica,* particularly when they're waving them in Ben Hart's direction, are just asking for trouble. He's lucky Ben didn't plug him dead center. He could have just as easily, and he wouldn't have lost any sleep over it."

There was a short silence. "I suppose," Cassie said, "that I ought to be used to—all of you by now. But I'm not. Ben is a dear. But he is also a throwback, an anachronism, a relic of an age that doesn't exist any longer."

The smile reappeared. "Now you're talking like an anthropologist, *chica.* And you're wrong. Unfortunately. It's an age that still does exist, only it isn't as much out in the open as it used to be." His voice softened. "You take care of yourself, hear? It won't be for much longer. I have to go." His expression softened. "I have a date."

"So?" There was a smile behind the single word. "With whom?"

"Grace Cathcart. We've decided we may have something in common after all."

"I will hold my breath." The smile in Cassie's voice was very plain. The line went dead.

Johnny hung up, pushed back his chair, and stood up. To Tony Lopez in the outside office, "I'm going out. I'll be near the car so the radio will reach me." Seeing the question plain in Tony's face, Johnny could not resist adding, "I'm going up the ski-basin road. To look at the fall color."

Tony, shaking his head slowly, watched Johnny until he disappeared. The *brujo,* the sorcerer, was at it again, he thought, and rolled his eyes toward the ceiling.

Grace Cathcart was punctual. She parked her Jaguar next to Johnny's pickup and got out gracefully, her face expressionless. She was dressed as before in tailored frontier trousers, polished boots, and a silk shirt. Over her shoulders she now wore a cashmere cardigan sweater against the chill of this 10,000-foot level.

"There's a bench just over here," Johnny said, "where we can talk." He left the window of his truck down in order to hear a radio call, and led the way. They sat, facing each other across the built-in picnic table. "You've heard what happened to Penny Lincoln?" Johnny said.

"There was an item in the paper this morning. Why do you ask, Lieutenant?"

"You can't guess?"

219

"I think it would be far better," Grace Cathcart said, "if you were to tell me what you would like to know, Lieutenant, instead of dropping hints."

Johnny nodded. "Penny Lincoln," he said, "was beaten at least partly because of you. I don't think the paper said that."

The smooth face remained expressionless, Johnny noted, but in the woman's eyes there was a sudden change. "You are not a very pleasant man," she said. "I suppose you know that?"

"I never set out to be a Boy Scout," Johnny said. "The kind of people I have to deal with usually don't deserve gentle treatment. You wanted me to be plain. All right. Penny Lincoln was beaten badly partly because of her association with Charley Harrington, and partly because of her association with you. Do you want me to be plainer than that?"

There was a change in Grace Cathcart's face then, a faint tightening of the flat muscles in her cheeks. And her eyes were angry. "My private associations, Lieutenant—"

"Would ordinarily be your own business," Johnny said. "Agreed. As I told Penny day before yesterday, I don't give a damn about your morals or hers, except, I said, that they might get her into trouble. They did. Bad trouble."

Grace Cathcart was silent for a few moments. She said at last, "Am I to understand that you believe I too am in danger?"

"Possible, but I doubt it. The two men who worked Penny over are where they won't bother anyone for a while. There could be others, but I don't think so."

The smooth face had regained its composure. "Then why did you want this meeting?"

The radio in the pickup came alive. Johnny cocked his head to listen briefly. "Not for me." He looked at Grace Cathcart again. "Why this meeting?" he said. "Just on the chance, slim, I admit, that you would tell me some of the things you and Penny talked about, during the relaxed time after—"

"There is no need to be coarse, Lieutenant." There was even a hint of color high in Grace's cheeks, quickly gone. "Whatever we may have talked about does not concern you in any way."

"I think it does," Johnny said. "Because the evidence seems to indicate that at least some of what you let Penny hear, probably without even realizing it, she passed on to Charley Harrington during *their* relaxed times. And she didn't think anything about it either."

"You talk in riddles," Grace Cathcart said. Her tone was cold. "What could I possibly have told Penny that would be of interest to the Harrington person?"

"Things about your husband's activities."

"That is absurd. I know nothing about my husband's activities. I told you that. I told Dr. Enright the same thing."

"Saying it," Johnny said, "doesn't make it so. Cassie didn't believe you, lady, and I don't either. You're not stupid. Maybe deliberately blind, but not stupid. You live with the man. In the same house. He has three telephones on his desk, and only one has a listed number. If you don't know all that he does, you can guess, and you don't like what you guess enough

221

that you went to see Cassie." Johnny paused. His eyes held hers. "And now have come up here to see me for the same reason."

"And what is that?"

"Because you're scared that somebody's going to lower the boom on your husband, and you don't want to have it land on you too, so you're trying to get clear and stay clear."

Grace Cathcart took her time, her eyes remaining steady on Johnny's face. She said at last, "You have quite a reputation in Santo Cristo, Lieutenant. Perhaps it is deserved. But in this instance you are wide of the mark."

"Am I?" Johnny shook his head. The woman was good, he thought. "I don't think so. But if that's the way you want it, that's how we'll leave it." He stood up from the bench. "For now," he said. "Thanks for coming up." He pointed. "Along that trail perhaps fifty yards is the best place to see the fall color. If you're interested. *Adiós.*"

Grace Cathcart sat where she was and watched while Johnny walked to his pickup, got in, and drove off. He did not look back.

He drove slowly and with care down the winding mountain road. Too often flatlanders visiting from Texas, Oklahoma, or Kansas, unused to mountain driving, took the turns too fast or swung too wide on blind curves, and it behooved those who knew better to drive defensively. And while he drove he went over his conversation with Grace Cathcart.

Despite her denials, he remained convinced of the accuracy of his reasoning. The vehemence of her protestations, in fact, had further convinced him that he was on the right track. Besides, it all fitted too well. There remained, he thought, only one or two loose ends to gather up, and he anticipated no great difficulty in doing that. He could give thought now to the best way to bring it all to a head.

Sam stopped by the Johnson Gallery on her way to opening her bar. Monica Jaramillo was rearranging the window display, and Sam watched her deft, sure movements for a little time in silence. "I had a talk with Johnny Ortiz," she said at last as Monica finished and turned back into the gallery room. "He has ideas, even if I don't know exactly what they are."

"About me?" Monica's expression was troubled.

"I don't think so," Sam said. "He asked me if you just worked here in the gallery, and I said as far as I knew you did."

"That is all I do."

Sam gestured around the gallery. "All this comes up from Mexico air freight to Albuquerque? And it goes through customs there?"

Monica nodded. "There is no duty on works of art, but, yes, it has to go through customs anyway." Her face was still troubled.

"Something you're not telling me?" Sam said.

Monica raised her slim shoulders and let them fall in a gesture of helplessness. "I don't *know* anything," she said.

"But you have ideas?"

There was hesitation. "I'm afraid so," Monica said.

Sam was thinking of Penny's naked, huddled body

223

on the floor of the tiny bedroom, and hearing again in her mind the small, whimpering sounds Penny had made. And this was none of her business, either, she told herself, but almost against her will the words still came out. "Do you want to tell me about them? It might be better."

Monica hesitated. "Let's have a cup of coffee," she said. "And we'll see."

Back in his office again, Johnny called the Harrington house. Lucille answered. "I've been thinking," Johnny said, "that it might be useful if you, one or both, were to go up to Charley's house and go through his papers. I'm asking a lot, I know, but it could be important."

There was no hesitation. "We will, of course," Lucille said. "Anything at all to help."

"I have the key here."

"We will come by immediately."

They were prompt. They sat in Johnny's office, and, as usual, Lucille took the lead. "If you could give us some idea of what we are looking for—"

"It's a little complicated," Johnny said, "and I'm guessing, but I think it adds up that Charley must have kept personal, and secret, financial records. He juggled his finances; that much seems clear. And even with his capabilities, I believe he must have needed records he could consult to see at any time exactly where he stood."

"Perhaps in his PC?" Waldo said. "His personal computer?"

Johnny nodded. "Could be."

Lucille disagreed. "Charley," she said, "was well-acquainted with the vulnerability of computers." She even managed a faint smile. "He himself demonstrated that they could be invaded. I believe that if we find anything, it will be a written record, perhaps in a code of some kind not easily broken."

She was speaking directly to Johnny now, and a slight hesitation accompanied by rapid blinking of her eyes indicated how painful the memories were. But her voice betrayed no emotion. "At one time," she said, "Charley was quite interested in cryptography. Among many other things." She added, "He and Waldo shared that interest. Waldo is a very good cryptologist too."

She rose from her chair then and accepted the key Johnny offered. Waldo rose with her. Still Lucille hesitated. "That . . . girl the other night," she said. "Penelope Lincoln, was it not? So she *was* in danger?"

"She was," Johnny said. "If I'd seen things a little more clearly—" He shook his head, and the anger in his eyes was plain. "But I didn't. In a way I warned her, but that wasn't enough. My fault."

"Admitting culpability," Lucille said, "is not always easy. Waldo and I are—finding that out." Her voice turned brisk again. "We will be in touch as soon as we find anything—if we do."

Tony Lopez came into the office, almost as if summoned by an inaudible signal. There was a sensitivity in Tony, Johnny had often thought, that defied analysis. Leaning now against the wall, Tony said, "Yes?" and waited quietly.

"A few things I want to find out," Johnny said. "Get out your notebook."

Tony sat down, pencil in hand. As expected, he thought, the *brujo* had seen visions again. And he could not refrain from asking one question: "How was the fall color?"

"Spectacular," Johnny said. He was smiling.

19

Ross Cathcart was in his study when Grace returned home that afternoon. The computer screen was dark, and all three phones were on their bases. "Where have you been?" Cathcart said. It was a demand. The man was obviously on edge.

"Seeing a man." Grace Cathcart's voice was expressionless. "And, incidentally, admiring the fall foliage on the ski-basin road."

"What man?"

"The police lieutenant."

Cathcart leaned back in his chair and his eyes searched her face. "Why?"

"He asked me to meet him."

"I mean, what did he want?"

"I assumed that was what you meant."

"Well?"

"He," Grace Cathcart said, "is more subtle than

227

you may think. His real purpose was to tell me to warn you that, in his phrase, 'Somebody is going to lower the boom on you.'"

"That," Cathcart said, "is ridiculous. I had nothing to do with Harrington's death. Not that I'm not happy it happened. But my hands are clean." He held them out, palms up, fingers spread as if to demonstrate their cleanliness.

Grace Cathcart studied him coldly. "In some ways, you have a limited mind," she said. "And you are greedy. That is a bad combination." She paused. "You are also badly frightened, and have been ever since you returned from Mexico City. I won't even bother to guess the precise reason. It no longer matters."

"And what does that mean?"

"I'm leaving you. I have been thinking about it for some time. I made the final decision driving down from the Aspen lookout."

"And you'll live on what?"

"This," Grace said, "is a community-property state. One-half of everything you possess belongs to me—this house, the gallery, the securities, commodity options and futures, everything. And I intend to collect it."

Cathcart sat silent for a few moments. His eyes had not left her face. "Like hell you will—"

"And," Grace Cathcart said, "you probably won't be needing money anyway. I expect you will be in no position to spend anything." She paused again as she had before to lend emphasis to her words. "In jail," she said.

It was then that one of the telephones on Cathcart's desk rang. His eyes still on his wife, Cathcart picked it up and spoke his name.

"Ortiz here," Johnny's voice said. "I want you here at police headquarters right away. If I have to I'll send someone, with a warrant, to bring you in."

Cathcart closed his eyes and took a deep breath. He let it out slowly. "That won't be necessary," he said. "I'll come."

"And you'd better bring your lawyer with you," Johnny said, and hung up.

Cathcart stood up. He tried to keep his voice under control, but his anger was plain. "The policeman," he said. "He wants me. What did you tell him? You—" He started to raise his hand.

"Strike me," Grace Cathcart said, "and if it's the last thing I do, I will kill you."

Ben Hart answered the phone in the big living room of the ranch house where he was sitting talking with Cassie. The foreman had gone back to his outside chores, and Ben had taken the precaution of sticking the .45 revolver in the waistband of his jeans. Cassie was unable to keep her eyes from it.

On the phone now Johnny said, "A little talk. In my office. I've invited a few guests. Care to come?"

The words bristled with overtones, Ben thought. "I wouldn't miss it," he said, and hesitated. "Shall I bring Cassie?"

"I think not," Johnny said. He had considered it, and made his decision before placing the call. "It could get . . . a little uncomfortable."

"Got it," Ben said. "Anything you want me to bring along?"

There was a smile in Johnny's voice. "Like that cannon of yours? No. That won't be necessary."

Ben nodded. "I'll be along directly." He hung up

the phone and looked at Cassie. "Sorry, honey, but the man says you stay here. Fred'll stay with you." He got to his feet and looked down from his great height. "We don't want anything to happen to you, and we'll see that it don't."

Cassie watched him go to the door, open it, and bellow for Fred. It was hard to believe that Ben was real, she thought as she had though before. Nothing in her life before she had come here to Santo Cristo, and to Johnny, had prepared her for men like Ben or Mark Hawley or, for that matter, for Johnny himself.

They were somehow make-believe, actors on film or on TV screen, except that they weren't. She could still recall vividly the scene she had witnessed last night leaning out over the gallery railing, old Ben with the big revolver in his fist looking at the wounded man almost with contempt as he told him not to bleed on the Indian rugs. Unbelievable.

"Here's Fred," Ben said from the door. "Bye, honey." He was gone, and in only a moment Cassie heard the dusty Cadillac monster Ben drove roar into life and charge off down the ranch driveway.

Lucille Harrington hung up the phone. From his desk Waldo said, "Do you think it wise for us both to attend this . . . conference?"

"Charley—" Lucille began, and there she stopped, and breathed deeply. "I am sorry," she said.

"I could go alone," Waldo said.

Lucille shook her head silently.

Waldo sighed. "Very well." His smile was sad. "When you have made up your mind, Lu—" He shook his head. "Very little can budge you."

Lucille swallowed, and gathered herself visibly. "You have finished working out Charley's notes?"

Waldo nodded. "Enough. And it is as we guessed. The funds did come from Cathcart. But exactly where they went . . ."

"I still do not believe it was simple avarice," Lucille said, her voice not quite steady. "He, Charley, was not greedy. He—"

"Easy, Lu." Waldo got up from his desk chair. "You are sure you want to go?"

"I am sure." Lucille's face was again composed. "And I am ready."

Mark Hawley said, "You reckon you have the whole story, son?" His eyes were on the far wall of his office, and the phone was propped with practiced ease between his shoulder and his cheek.

"Near enough," Johnny said. "I thought you might like to sit in."

"You better believe it. The Feds have been at me most of the day."

"I think you'll have a couple of bones to throw them," Johnny said.

"Respect for authority was never your long suit, was it, son?" The congressman was smiling; it was his crocodile-in-the-shallows smile. "As far as that goes, it was never mine either. I'll be right along."

"I want some papers," Johnny told Tony Lopez, "official-looking papers. I'll sit over there at the table, and I want them spread out."

"*Entendido,* understood," Tony said, although he had no idea what the *brujo* was up to now. "And me?"

"I don't *think* I'll need you."

This at least Tony could understand. "But just in case—" he said.

"Yes. In the next room, I think."

"Bueno."

Cathcart arrived first, alone. He looked around at the arrangement of chairs, and then at Johnny behind the library table. "Joe Whitney is coming," Cathcart said, and sat down. He seemed unable to keep his hands quiet. From time to time he glanced at Johnny, who was studying the papers before him in total silence.

Mark Hawley walked in, along with Ben Hart. Mark too looked around at the chairs and nodded. "Expecting a full house, son?" he said.

Johnny looked up from the papers then. "More or less," he said, and went back to his studying as Hawley took the chair next to Ben.

Grace Cathcart appeared in the doorway, composed as always. "Was I invited, Lieutenant?"

"No," Johnny said, "but you are welcome to sit in."

Ben Hart and Mark Hawley were on their feet. "Take this chair, ma'am," Ben said, and pulled one forward from the wall.

"Front row center," Mark Hawley said, "just like in London."

Cathcart's head came up and he stared briefly at the congressman before he looked away again.

Grace Cathcart said, "Thank you," and seated herself with her usual accomplished smooth facility.

Lucille and Waldo Harrington arrived, and again both Ben Hart and the congressman stood up. Lucille smiled at them, and at Johnny. She and Waldo sat together at one end of the semicircle of chairs.

"Well," Johnny said, looking around, "I think we might as well begin. Unless—?" He looked at Cathcart.

"I would like my attorney present," Cathcart said, and watched Johnny nod assent.

"I sort of thought you would," Johnny said, "so we'll wait a bit." He went back to his papers.

Joseph Whitney arrived. He was breathing hard. "Sorry I'm late. I was delayed."

"No problem," Johnny said, and leaned back in his chair, his left hand relaxed on the tabletop, his right resting quietly on his thigh. "So now we can start." He paused. "It's a tangled tale, and you'll just have to bear with me while I lay it out." He looked around at them all. "Okay?"

"You have the floor, son," the congressman said as if he were addressing a congressional witness. "Proceed."

There was a general murmur of assent.

Johnny's eyes were on Lucille Harrington. He spoke quietly, and made no gestures. "With apologies," he began, "the starting place was Charley Harrington's death. Everything stems from that."

Lucille inclined her head in a small nod of understanding. Her face was composed.

"I won't labor the facts," Johnny said, "but he was killed with a shotgun loaded with double-ought shot. He was killed in his own house by someone who was waiting for him. That someone cleaned up the tile floor and the wall of the passageway, took Charley's body to an arroyo, and left it there where it was discovered by some boys searching for a lost dog."

He looked around at them all then, his face as if

233

carved in stone. "That," he said again, "was our starting place. But it was not the beginning. A man named Glenn Ronson had already been killed, also by a shotgun blast, and his body had been driven out to Ben Hart's ranch where it was left inside the fence line, not far from the ranch drive. Glenn Ronson had been house-sitting for the Cathcarts, who *had been* on vacation in Scotland and England." He emphasized the past-perfect tense.

Ross Cathcart stirred uneasily. "We were still on vacation when all of this happened," he said. "We didn't get back until both men were dead."

"Maybe," Johnny said. "But we'll get back to that."

Joseph Whitney said, "I believe we would like an explanation of your obvious hint, Lieutenant. My client maintains that he and his wife had not returned, but you seem to be disputing that. Will you explain?"

Johnny thought about it. He nodded. *"Bueno.* When I visited the Cathcart house and spoke with Mrs. Cathcart—this was after Mr. Cathcart had gone down to Mexico City—she, Mrs. Cathcart, told me the names of some of the plays they had seen in London after they had finished fishing in Scotland. One of the plays was a Shaw revival."

He paused and looked at Grace Cathcart. "But the Shaw revival," Johnny said, "had already closed before you got to London—*if* you actually went into London at all. We are checking that now, but my guess is that you flew from Scotland, Edinburgh perhaps, to Heathrow Airport which is outside London, and there took a flight back to the States. As I say we are checking on that now. The airlines are cooperating. Thanks to Congressman Hawley."

Ross Cathcart looked at Grace. He said nothing, but his anger was plain. Grace Cathcart's face remained expressionless.

"But leaving opportunity aside," Johnny said, "we still need motive. The fact that both men were killed by shotgun blast, double-ought buckshot in both cases, would tend to indicate that the same person was responsible. Double-ought buckshot is quite rare. No store in Santo Cristo, for example, even carries it. Not too long ago it was fairly common, but not now."

"No need for it," Ben Hart said. "You shoot even a bird big as a goose with it, and there wouldn't be enough meat left to bother with." He glanced at Lucille. "Sorry, ma'am."

Lucille nodded, and her lips formed the words, "It's all right," but no sound came out.

In the silence, "Charley Harrington," Johnny said, "was—remarkable is the only word. Even as a kid, he was something quite special. A loner, and it's no wonder he didn't have any close friends. Other kids couldn't even begin to keep up with him. Maybe that's why he did some of the things he did, I don't know. He—"

"He was trying to impress us," Lucille Harrington said, "Waldo and me. We *were* impressed by him, but I'm afraid he didn't believe it." She stopped there, and sat quiet, looking straight ahead, unseeing.

Johnny said, "Charley killed a man with his car. I thought maybe there might have been something in that, some old grudge, but it didn't fit, and, besides, the killing was strictly an accident." He paused thoughtfully.

"Like I said," he went on after a few moments, "Charley did a lot of things that were unusual. Everybody knows about his CH Company that started in his garage. His parents know, because they were brought into it after the fact, that Charley provided his own financing in a very special way we don't need to go into now." He shook his head faintly. "Or maybe it's better if we do. Charley arranged financing through the bank, not in the usual way, but by tapping into the bank's computer system, setting up a dummy account, and having money put into it. He did that several times, whenever he needed more money. Each time the bank caught up with him he was in a position to pay it back, with interest. And since the bank didn't want any of that kind of publicity, it wasn't made public."

Ben Hart was grinning openly. "Hell of a smart kid. I never did like banks."

Grace Cathcart said, "Is all of this germane?"

"Yes, it is," Johnny said. "I told you it was a tangled tale. I also said that Charley didn't have any friends, close friends. That wasn't quite true. He did have one friend, somebody who took him for what he was, something very much out of the ordinary, and treated him the way Charley wanted to be treated—with respect. I'm reading between the lines, but I think it had to be something like that. Sid Thomas, the painter, who is older than anybody here, and Charley Harrington the kid were close friends, very close."

Lucille Harrington closed her eyes. When she opened them again, they were bright with tears. She said nothing and made no move.

"Charley," Johnny said, "would sit and watch Sid paint. And he'd ask questions, not kid questions, but questions most grown-ups even if they appreciated art wouldn't even think to ask—how can you show a whole big mountain on a piece of canvas so small? How come you exaggerate that corner or that curve— and yet it looks more real that way? That kind of thing." Johnny shook his head. "They even talked about far-out mathematics, at least Charley did, because he understood it. Sid didn't know what he was talking about, but in a way they communicated."

The room was still, and Johnny himself was silent for a few moments. "Will Carston," he said, "told me that Robert Oppenheimer, the atomic bomb man, was interested, just as Charley was, in far-out Oriental religions that somehow had something to do with mathematics. Don't ask me for particulars. I don't even try to understand. But somehow Sid Thomas talking about art, and Charley Harrington talking about what he knew, were on the same wavelength."

He stopped again. The room was silent. "Sometime during all this," Johnny said, "something happened that wouldn't seem to have anything to do with Charley—but it did. Sid Thomas had a show at a gallery, the Johnson Gallery, which Ross Cathcart owns."

Joseph Whitney stirred in his chair. "I object, Lieutenant. This cannot be germane, and I—"

"This isn't a court of law, counselor," Johnny said. "And you'll have your say when I'm done. Not before." He made no move, no gesture with either hand, but he dominated the room, and Whitney was silent.

"So," Johnny said after a moment, "Sid had this show. Sid isn't very cagey when it comes to money. He's never cared much about it, and he's never paid much attention to it. But he got skinned at that show, and he found out about it later. The Johnson Gallery had one price for the customers who bought the paintings, and a lot of them did, and another, lower price to tell Sid about when they paid him what they said was his share."

"That," Cathcart said, "is an out-and-out lie. It—"

"I doubt it," Johnny said, "but it doesn't matter here. And again, with the congressman's help, we'll find out the truth. The records are still there."

"Easy enough," Mark Hawley said. "The Treasury folks are already poking into it. Among other things."

Cathcart opened his mouth and closed it again silently. He took a deep breath. To Whitney he said, "Do I have to sit and listen to this, Joe? They're pillorying me, and—"

"Just sit still and be quiet," Johnny said. "You'll have your say." And again his voice dominated the room. "I said it doesn't matter here, and it doesn't. What does matter is that Sid *thought* he'd been skinned, and so did Charley Harrington, his friend. That was the important thing."

Mark Hawley was frowning now. "You going to explain that, son?"

"I am," Johnny said. "Because it's the key to just about everything that happened." He took his time. "Here's this kid, this exceptional kid who's able to invent things nobody else can think of, and who can hornswoggle the bank out of money to pay for developing his inventions just about whenever he wants to—and his friend, his only real, close friend gets himself cheated." He paused again. "Charley wasn't about to take that lying down." He looked at Cathcart. "From that time on," he said, "you were in trouble, bad trouble. Charley tapped your phone. All three phones, as a matter of fact, *and* your computer. For the record, they're still tapped."

"I've had them checked," Cathcart said. "An expert. And they're not tapped. He said—"

"A moment." Lucille Harrington's voice was calm and authoritative. This was no longer the mother speaking, this was the world-class physicist explaining patiently, as to a congressional committee composed of nontechnical people, precisely what was and was not true. "You may be assured, Mr. Cathcart, that your telephone lines and your computer are indeed tapped. The technician who came to see you was not a technician at all. He is one of the world's foremost physicists, a friend of Waldo's and mine, specializing in electronics." She smiled faintly. "He is also what he calls 'a tinkerer,' and he reported that this was the most ingenious tap he had ever encountered, one that would certainly defy any routine examination."

Cathcart sat still and silent, but his color had changed and his breathing was no longer steady. Suddenly he sprang to his feet and shouted, "You can't—"

Ben Hart reached out with one big hand, caught Cathcart's arm, and flung him back into his chair. "Sit down and shut up," Ben said. "Let the man talk. He told you you'd have your say." He looked at Johnny. "Go on," he said.

Johnny nodded. "Charley Harrington learned a lot of things about you," he said to Cathcart. "Some of it he didn't care about—at first. He was after only one thing—money, in order to get even for what you did by cheating Sid Thomas out of his fair share of the picture sales. That was his paramount motive. He wasn't after your money for himself. He could always tap the bank again. He wanted your money for Sid."

Again he paused and looked around the silent room. "And he got it. You don't know it, but you donated anonymously almost every Sid Thomas canvas that hangs in the Fine Arts Museum, and the money for those paintings, at prices Charley set, went into Sid's pocket. Precisely how he managed to get your money I don't know, but—"

"We do," Waldo Harrington said. "It's all there in Charley's notes. In code. You were right. He had to keep a record because his methods were so complicated. But the trail is plain." He looked at Lucille. "You were right," he said, and smiled.

Johnny looked at Lucille too. She was smiling through tears that had again appeared, smiling and nodding happily. "I knew it was not sheer avarice," she said. "He—Charley wasn't—greedy. Not that way."

"He had his own way of doing things," Johnny said gently, "but his motives were sound. He was simply punishing what he saw as a dirty trick on Cathcart's part." He paused, and his voice turned cold again. "But that was only part of it." He looked around the room and let the sentence hang in the air.

"*Bueno,*" he said at last. "I said he didn't care *at first* about some of what he found out about you." He was looking straight at Cathcart, who seemed to have shrunk in size as well as confidence. "But later, after he thought about it, maybe when he was a little older, wiser, he saw the full implications. That was when he went back to Washington"—he was looking now at

Mark Hawley—"and had that dinner with you, and that long talk. I'm guessing what he told you, but it had to do with Cathcart, probably cocaine coming up from Colombia, ways and means and the violence that went along with it. *Es verdad?*"

"You guess pretty good, son," the congressman said.

"There is always money involved," Johnny said. "Large sums of money. In cash. It was always in cash, by the way, that Charley gave the money to the museum for the purchase of Sid's paintings."

Joseph Whitney said, "My client and I have listened with considerable patience, I believe, to a great deal of—"

"I'm not finished," Johnny said, again in that tone that demanded, and got, full attention. "Now," he said, "we come right back to where we started—two murders. And a girl beaten up badly, a man attempting to break into Charley's house, and another man trying to get at Cassie Enright. It's all part of the same thing. I'll lay that out for you too."

He took his time, setting his thoughts in order. They all watched him and waited. "The Cathcart house had been ransacked when the Cathcarts *allegedly* returned home."

"Damn it—!" Ross Cathcart began.

"I told you to shut up," Ben Hart said, and there was no mistaking the threat in the old man's voice. "I won't tell you again."

Cathcart was silent.

"I said allegedly," Johnny said, "because once we found that the Shaw play had closed before the Cathcarts could have seen it, and the possibility was clear that they might have come back sooner—soon enough, maybe, to have had a great deal to do with the murders—then the ransacked house could have been just something dragged across the trail to confuse." He had their full attention and he let the silence grow and stretch. "Nothing in the house was damaged, and nothing was taken, both of which made the false trail theory more likely. Except for one thing." Again he paused.

Johnny looked around at the faces—Lucille and Waldo, Grace Cathcart, Ben Hart, Mark Hawley, Cathcart, and Whitney. "Cathcart," Johnny said, "collapsed with atrial fibrillations—heart flutter that landed him in the hospital's CCU—coronary care unit. Why? There were two possibilities. First, the early return from England and whatever happened here as a result of that early return was just too much for him to take. Or, second, even though nothing was destroyed in the house, and nothing was *said* to have been taken, something *was* missing, and it was something that upset Cathcart very badly, enough to put him in the hospital."

Whitney stirred again. "You talk in riddles—" he began.

"Not really," Johnny said. "What could have been taken that was that important? Well, things began to fall into place." He raised his left hand, fingers spread. "First, as soon as Cathcart was out of the hospital he hustled off to Mexico City. Why? Second, you, Congressman, warned me off Cathcart and put the Feds on me when I tried to follow him. That pointed right at Cathcart's involvement in something illegal—like dope? Third, Cassie went to Mexico City in my place and was . . . not roughed-up, but was given a bad time and it was obvious she was threatened, and both she and Cathcart came back here scared.

"It almost had to add up to money," Johnny went on. "It was the only thing that fitted. Money that had been in Cathcart's possession, that didn't belong to him—at least not all of it did—and that was missing from the ransacked house.

"Given that," he said after a pause, "it all made sense. Cathcart would *have* to say nothing was missing because the money was illegal. And the fact that it *was* missing was enough to put him in the hospital. Then when he got out, he had to rush off to Mexico City to explain that the money was gone, that it had been stolen, and that he didn't even have any idea who had taken it."

The room was dead silent. Cathcart sat like a man in shock, staring straight ahead, almost rigid, his face devoid of color.

"Cathcart's story of the theft of the money was not believed in Mexico City," Johnny said, "at least not taken as the complete truth. And Cassie's presence was taken as some kind of threat. That had to mean that the people in Mexico City knew who Cassie was, who I was—because Cassie's phone call to me from San Antonio was specific in its request that I not meet the plane. And by building out from that—"

"Extrapolation," Lucille Harrington said, and nodded.

Johnny smiled briefly and nodded. "Yes, that's the word. By extrapolating from what we knew, we could assume that someone here in Santo Cristo was keeping Mexico City informed of the who and the what and the why." He looked around at them all. "Clear so far?"

The room remained silent.

"Bueno," Johnny said. "Charley Harrington had seen that the girl Penny Lincoln might be in some danger because of her relationship to him. Whether he also knew of her relationship with Grace Cathcart, I don't know, but I think he must have, because he had probably learned some things about Cathcart from Penny, which is why he thought she might be in danger, and she could only have learned them from Grace Cathcart."

Grace Cathcart sat quiet, looking straight ahead, her face composed.

"Two men were on that plane from Mexico City," Johnny said. "They may have boarded it at San Antonio, I don't know that yet, but, again, the congressman is having that checked. They were looking for the trail of the money that had disappeared from Cathcart's house, and they went straight for Penny Lincoln. I ought to have foreseen that, and I didn't. My fault. That's why she is in the hospital now." His face showed its harsh lines, and for a moment or two the flat muscles in his cheeks moved angrily.

"Next," Johnny said, "they made the mistakes of going to search Charley Harrington's house, where I was waiting, and going to work over Cassie as they had Penny Lincoln—but Ben Hart was waiting." He paused. "My man admitted that it was money they were after, quite a bit of money—some hundreds of thousands of dollars in cash."

Ben Hart blew out his cheeks in a silent whistle. "High rollers," he said.

"Very high," Johnny said. "But the trail was cold, and they were following the wrong scent. The real trail led in a different direction. It had nothing to do with Charley Harrington—at least not directly." With his left hand he rubbed his chin reflectively as he chose his words.

"The real trail began with the first murder—Glenn Ronson. He was the house-sitter for the Cathcarts. He had sat for them before. When his body was found, his wallet with a little money and identification was nearby. His keys were not. I think we can assume that he was killed for his keys, among them the keys to Cathcart's house. That way, with Ronson dead and the Cathcarts still gone, somebody had ample time to search the house for the money he knew was there. How did he know it? That was a good question that took a little time to figure out, but the answer—when it came—was plain enough." Once more he looked slowly around the room. Nobody moved.

Johnny nodded, satisfied that he had their complete attention. "Charley Harrington might have known about that money because he still had that tap on Cathcart's phones," he said. "In fact, Charley Harrington did know about it. So did someone else. That someone *could* have known because he had connections in Mexico City which might mean that he was also Mexico City's source of information about who Cassie was, and about me, hence the warning for me to stay away from the plane coming from San Antonio. That was one possible answer. There was also another." He rubbed his chin reflectively again with his left hand as if considering whether or not to explain that last comment.

"The other possible answer was that the someone knew about the money in Cathcart's house because Charley Harrington had told him." He paused once more. "There was only one person Charley would logically have told that." He was looking now at Whitney. "You, Counselor. He trusted you and went to you for guidance in complicated matters that were outside of his range of knowledge, financial matters. He might well have told you things about Cathcart, no?"

Whitney shook his head. "He didn't. And if he had, I wouldn't have listened. Ross Cathcart is also my client."

"And yet," Johnny said, "you came to me with more than hints of money changing hands between Cathcart and Charley. You were careful to say you didn't know all of the facts and didn't want to know—as an attorney, an officer of the court. But you did know. So I think it makes sense that you might also have known of the large cache of money in Cathcart's house. And the Cathcarts were gone. Why not search the house, find the money, and take it? After tearing the house apart to make it look like a burglary? Its loss would not be reported, you could be sure of that."

Whitney was smiling. "Your imagination is running away with you, Lieutenant. It—"

"That first possibility I mentioned," Johnny said as if Whitney had not spoken, "the possibility that the someone who knew of the money in Cathcart's possession because he was the link to Mexico City could also apply. The telephone call Cassie was told to make in San Antonio was obviously set up to give someone the knowledge of the plane's arrival time in Albuquerque so it could be met. And you were there to meet it. Coincidence? I think not."

"I told you, Lieutenant, that I was meeting a friend—"

"Inocencio Valdez, yes," Johnny said, "who lives in El Paso, you said. But Inocencio Valdez does not live in El Paso. He lives in San Antonio. The congressman had that checked. It begins to look more and more as if your meeting that plane was not quite as innocent— no pun intended with your friend's name—as you would have us believe because Valdez flew back to San Antonio the next day; presumably his mission, his meeting with you, accomplished. I don't like coincidence, Counselor."

Whitney was smiling no longer. He was angry. It was clear. "You are making insinuations I resent, Lieutenant, and I will not—"

"And we get back to double-ought buckshot," Johnny said. "Remember? It's scarce. I had Tony Lopez check. The only person who ever used it as far as Tony knew, he told me, was a fellow who ran sheep over near Pecos. A fellow named Rael, Esteban Rael. What's your middle name, Counselor? The initial is *R,* and the full name is in the court records—Joseph Rael Whitney. Was there any possible connection? I put Tony to looking into it, and it turns out that there is. He is your *primo,* your cousin, no? Another coincidence?"

"This is absurd," Whitney said. "Guesswork upon hypothesis upon supposition—all adding up to nothing. Nothing at all! I will not—!"

"One more item," Johnny said, "and it gets to the

heart of the problem. Why was Charley Harrington killed? By the same method that was used to kill Ronson the house-sitter, and presumably by the same hand. There is only one logical explanation, and that is because Charley would have guessed who had killed Ronson, the house-sitter, and why; just as soon as the alleged burglary of the Cathcart house was discovered, Charley would have pointed the finger, and that—"

"Basta! Enough!" Whitney's voice was harsh now, and a gun had appeared in his hand. He held it loosely with practiced ease. He started to rise—

"Just stay where you are," Johnny said. "And put the gun down. I've had a gun pointed at your belly for the last half-hour."

Whitney looked at the arm that had remained below the tabletop. He looked at Johnny. "You're bluffing. And I'm—" He stopped there.

Johnny was smiling. It was not a pleasant smile. "Try me," he said.

The room was still. Whitney's mouth opened and then closed again soundlessly. He licked his lips and took a deep breath, but remained frozen in his half-risen position, obviously unsure, unable to move. Then slowly, as if under compulsion against which there was no defense, his knees began to flex until he was again sitting tensely on the chair.

"Put the gun down," Johnny said. "Slowly and carefully."

Whitney hesitated. Slowly he bent forward, laid the gun on the floor, and straightened again with care. His eyes had not left Johnny's face.

"Pick it up, Ben," Johnny said, and Ben took the

gun from the floor, held it in his big hand, snorted contemptuously at its size, and stuck it in the waistband of his jeans.

Johnny brought his right hand out from behind the table. It was empty. "Tony!" he said. "I think you can come in now. We've got a guest for that empty cell."

Epilogue

They sat in Ben Hart's big ranch living room with its huge picture window giving a stunning view of the great mountains still glowing gold with aspen color—Ben, Mark Hawley, Johnny, and Cassie.

"Speaking as the lawyer I was once upon a time," the congressman said, "the state is going to have a row to hoe pinning the two murders on Joe Whitney." He had a sip of Ben's whiskey and nodded appreciatively. "On the other hand," he said, "diligent search ought to turn up sufficient evidence to convince even the most skeptical jury." He looked hard at Johnny. "You didn't make up that part about Estéban Rael being Joe Whitney's cousin?"

Johnny shook his head. "One of those things that sometimes falls into your lap—Tony's mentioning a man who used double-ought buckshot to deal with coyotes, and remembering his name." He shrugged. "It came to me when I was in the shower—Whitney's middle initial was *R,* and when it fitted, then everything else fell into place."

Cassie closed her eyes briefly. "It's all over then?" she said.

"Mostly," Johnny said. "A few loose ends." He looked at Mark Hawley. "A woman named Monica Jaramillo, works at the Johnson Gallery, Cathcart's gallery. I think she'll be able to tell your Feds a few things."

"Such as?"

"I'm guessing," Johnny said, "but she was nervous about a couple of sculptures on display. They look like bronze castings, but they aren't. They're bronze powder in plastic, polymer, I think, whatever that is. The point is that they are big, and light because they're hollow. She handles them when she arranges the displays. If she noticed a change in their weight, as I think she may have, she might figure that something had been taken out of them. Maybe some pounds of cocaine? Her mind might run in that direction. Roberto Lewis, the fellow she lived with, now in jail, worked for Cathcart and traveled down into Mexico a lot. She might have put all that together, because it scared her when I showed up."

"We'll see," the congressman said. "It makes sense."

Ben Hart said, "You were sure as hell right when you said it was all tangled. The whole thing put its tail in its mouth and rolled around like a hoop." He shook his head sadly. "And all because a kid, Charley Harrington, had only one friend, Sid Thomas, old enough to be his grandfather." He finished his whis- key, sighed deeply, and looked at Mark Hawley. "Tastes like another," he said.

Hawley held out his glass. "I concur."

Johnny stood up. He held out his hand and Cassie took it. "Let's go home, *chica,*" Johnny said.

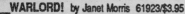